The Sheikh's Defiant Princess
Mel Teshco

MEL TESHCO

The Sheikh's Defiant Princess
Copyright © 2022 Mel Teshco
ALL RIGHTS RESERVED

Cover Art by HelzKat Designs
https://www.helzkatdesigns.com/

Chapter One

Sheikha Aisha Al Wahed's birthday party was in full swing by the time she was finally able to excuse herself and go in search of Tabari Usamah. Her jaw clenched. Trust her to want the one man on the planet who appeared to not return the favor. His rejection grated on her nerves and frayed her ego even as it made her more determined than ever to make him notice her.

Ugh. She could have almost any man she wanted, yet no one interested her the same way Tabari did.

What about the one other man on the planet who ties your insides up in knots and leaves you seething?

She lifted her chin. She wouldn't think about *him.* Sheikh Dhamar Qadir might be darkly handsome and richer than sin but he was more aggravating than a mosquito buzzing around her head in the dark. That he happened to be every other woman's fantasy didn't bear thinking about. Besides his looks and his wealth, what did they see in him?

That either one of those things was enough for most women just made her resent him more. Let them have him! Tabari was more than enough man for her.

Her whole body clenched. No doubt from the eclectic mix of traditional and pop songs that poured out of the outdoor speakers placed discreetly behind palm trees and water features, even in the half-dozen pools that guests used on the small but exclusive Holly Island, which her brother, Sheikh Hamid, had recently bought and renamed after his wife.

To most people, the island would be considered an extravagant wedding present that he'd gifted her, but Aisha knew better. After everything Holly had gone through in the desert with Hamid, she deserved nothing but the very best.

Aisha released a long breath. Maybe that was her problem? She'd led a relatively uneventful life, a young sheikha whose only dilemma had been the expectation of her people to act the part of a refined, dignified woman when beneath it all she wanted only to throw off the weight of all that judgement and emerge from her cocoon like a transformed butterfly, light and beautiful and floating on air.

"Happy birthday, Aisha!"

She smiled at yet another partygoer, the woman all but a stranger to her. But then, thanks to Aisha's sheltered life, she had no more than a handful of friends. Most of those invited here were little more than acquaintances. She'd hardly even seen her best friend, Zania.

For the moment though she was focused on finding Tabari. He was here somewhere; she'd damn well invited him. That he hadn't had the decency to put in an appearance after her brother had flown him—along with most of the other guests who'd been on her invite list—to this private island for her week-long, birthday celebrations added another fray to her unraveling emotions.

"Looking for someone?"

Her stomach rolled at the rich, dark voice that vibrated with suppressed amusement along with something not quite tangible. For just one second she allowed her lips to compress, her facial muscles to tighten. Then she looked up at her nemesis with a wide smile and an open, relaxed expression. "Sheikh Dhamar, how...lovely to see you."

That he was arguably one of the richest men on the planet, and one of the handsomest to boot irritated her beyond all reason. His tall, powerful physique, his smug and knowing, gorgeous dark-honey eyes made her want to irritate him ten times more in return.

"Enough with the formalities, Aisha," he murmured. "Just Dhamar is fine."

"Well, then, *Just Dhamar,* if you'll excuse me, I'm a little busy."

He smiled back, his teeth a dazzling white against the dark shadow of his designer stubble. "Too busy even to chat with one of your VIP guests?"

The last of her patience dissolved like mist on desert sand, and she snorted inelegantly. "Is *that* what you call yourself now?" Before he had a chance to answer, she added, "Why is it that every time I turn around *you're* there?"

"Yet every time you go sniffing around looking for Tabari he is nowhere to be found."

She narrowed her eyes, his words stinging far more than what hers would have stung him. He was insufferable! Not to mention rude and unapologetic. "I don't go 'sniffing' around anyone."

"Oh? Then you won't need me to tell you where I last saw him."

Her ears all but twitched. When a grin stretched his mouth even wider it took everything she had just to stay outwardly calm. The bastard was baiting her! It didn't stop her from asking, "You saw him?"

He nodded. "A few minutes ago, actually." He sighed, then clasped her arm "This way, *princess.*"

His nickname infuriated her almost as much as his fingers that warmed her skin and his rich scent of mahogany and ocean tang that filled her lungs. He was a womanizer and knew all the right tricks to make a woman's body betray her.

She stiffened, becoming an immobile statue as she fought against the attraction. "I'm quite sure I can find Tabari myself."

"Doubtful." He nodded toward her security team who watched them closely and were about to follow. "You will never be fully alone, princess. But maybe with me as your escort they'll give you some leeway."

"And why would they trust you?"

"I'm a sheikh aren't I?" He smiled conspiratorially. "And I'm a friend of your brother's. That has to mean something."

He waved a lazy hand at her team, relaying for them to stay put. When they looked at one another, then did as he asked, her chest tightened. How nice to be a man, and one so powerfully rich that no one had the audacity to ignore his command.

"What on earth are you trying to prove?" she asked.

"I'm not trying to prove anything other than to open your eyes."

"My eyes are already well and truly open as far as you are concerned."

"A shame the same can't be said for those rose-colored lenses you wear for Tabari."

It was odd how her legs took on a mind of their own and allowed Dhamar to guide her away from her own party and along a smooth, rock pathway between lush gardens that featured the spear-shaped, tropical orange flowers, bird of paradise. The path soon led them past the front of two and three bedroom guest lodgings with ocean views, where the sweet scent of frangipani competed with a salt-laden ocean breeze.

She stuck her nose in the air and inhaled appreciatively. "Actually, I see Tabari for the gentleman he really is."

"Then I must apologize in advance for your rude awakening."

She glared up at him, doing her best to ignore his demi-god appearance. "Does it really kill you to just once not be the center of a woman's attention?"

His nostrils flared. "Is that what you think this is about? My wounded ego?"

They rounded a corner and came into view of a garden courtyard. Aisha froze, her eyes going round and her mouth agape at the spectacle in front of her. Tabari's silver hair glinted under the afternoon sun, his legs spread wide to accommodate the diminutive height of the woman he passionately kissed.

Zania.

Aisha's breath caught in the back of her throat, her heart plummeting to her feet. That the woman was Aisha's best friend, the same friend who knew of Aisha's deep feelings for Tabari, caused the scene to swim in front of her eyes like a bad dream.

Dhamar's hold on her forearm gentled as he drew her away. "You've seen enough."

It was only once they'd walked a few hundred yards away that she found the strength to jerk her arm free. Her mouth drier than parchment, she gritted out, "I hope you're satisfied now."

"You left me with no choice." He exhaled roughly. "You're pining after the wrong man, Aisha. Everyone can see it but you."

"Let me guess, *this* is your birthday present to me." Her voice wobbled. "What did I ever do for you to hate me so much?"

His stare glinted with something raw and primal. "I don't hate you, Aisha."

Her hands clenched. "Only a man without a soul could possibly hurt someone so much."

He blinked, then swore savagely. "You'd rather find out about Tabari's infidelity months—*years*—from now? I did you a favor." He thrust a hand through his short, cropped dark hair. "You could have anyone you wanted."

"Yeah, anyone *but* the one man I want."

"You're a smart girl. You must know there are far better men out there for you than him."

"I see what you're doing, Dhamar. You hate me. You always have. And for whatever reason you're willing to make my life miserable—"

He stepped forward, dragged her close, then clapped his mouth over hers, cutting off any further accusation while making her gasp with shock. Mostly that her body immediately responded before her mind had time to process his audacity.

Heaven have mercy, his lips were soft yet insistent, his hands that cupped her face and kept her in place a pillar of strength that both kept her upright while draining her of willpower all at the same time.

Then he pulled back and said hoarsely, "Happy birthday, princess." His eyes held hers. "For the record, I don't hate you." His stare glowed as he glanced at her kiss-moistened lips. "Quite the opposite."

Chapter Two

Aisha was stunned into silence as she watched Dhamar pivot, then stride away, his masculine body in his dark pants, sky-blue shirt and fitted dark jacket cutting a striking figure. And despite all she'd seen, all she could think about was the rightness of his lips on hers. All she could hear on repeat were his last words. *I don't hate you. Quite the opposite.*

Why did that fill her with such...yearning? Had seeing Tabari making out with another woman made her want another man entirely? Was she seriously that fickle?

A nearby wooden bench caught her eye and she plopped down on it while watching the ocean in front of her change from light to dark blue before it blazed with streaks of reddish-orange as the sun began to disappear behind the horizon. Solar lights lit up the gardens and pathways with artificial, but soft light, giving the area a dreamy appearance.

A pity she wasn't feeling particularly dreamy. Her emotions were frazzled, her thoughts tangled up into knots.

"There you are."

She looked up at Tabari as he walked toward her, his handsome, weathered face creasing into a smile while one of his hands lifted to touch his mussed silver hair. He sat beside her, his tall, gym-toned body relaxed and loose beside her, the scent of sex and Zania's expensive perfume—the exact same perfume Aisha had bought her best friend for her twentieth birthday last month—clinging to him. *Ugh.* Did he realize a corner of his mouth had lipstick on it?

Clearly not. The man was about as carefree and unrepentant as one could get.

"What is my birthday girl doing out here all alone?" he asked, his warm hand landing on her thigh.

Her skin prickled beneath her bright lime-green gown. But then no amount of fabric could now disguise her revulsion at his touch.

"I'm nobody's girl," she refuted through gritted teeth. It wasn't until she pulled her leg away from his clasp that he looked at her with a faint frown.

"Look, I'm sorry I've been busy and haven't been immersed in your celebrations. I know how important today is to you. But I'm here now, aren't I?"

"Oh, I'm sure you were busy," she managed, somehow withholding a sneer at his slightly wheedling tone.

He blinked, and for the first time she noticed a number of his lashes were gray, his brow furrowed with deep creases. Their age difference had never bothered her, she'd liked that he was experienced in life. But perhaps their twenty-seven year age gap wasn't the only difference between them that was too great to overcome? He clearly had no scruples screwing her best friend before sitting beside Aisha like she was important to him, like they meant something together.

"I'm never too busy for you, Aisha."

She squeezed her eyes closed. *Liar!* He was so busy making out with her best friend, and no doubt screwing her, too, that not even her birthday had mattered. She swallowed convulsively. Why hadn't she noticed his easy deception? And why couldn't he treat her with the same care and attentiveness as Dhamar?

Dhamar might prickle her defenses but there was no denying his single-minded intensity. She felt like she was the only woman in the world whenever he was near. She had no doubt it was yet another reason women flocked to him like flamingoes to a fish-laden lake.

Tabari sighed heavily, as though her emotions were nothing short of a burden. "You look upset."

"Do I?" she asked, her words as empty as the void filling her up inside.

He shuffled closer, his cloying warmth now overburdening her senses. He looked around, as if to confirm they were alone at last with none of her security team in sight. "I'm sorry I haven't celebrated your birthday with you. But let me make it up to you? I have some aged scotch in my room." He smiled and winked. "It's also well-known for its medicinal purposes."

She snorted, aware she would have fallen for his suggestion not even an hour earlier. Now she was nothing short of repulsed. Dhamar had ripped off the blindfolds from her eyes, forcing her to see Tabari for the lowlife he really was. "Surely at your age fucking my best friend would be enough sex for one day?"

He stiffened, then spluttered. "I have no idea what you're—"

"I saw you with Zania!" She jerked to her feet and spun around to face him, her mind spinning even faster while her body was a stiff as a plank. "Give my *best friend* my regards."

He reached out, his hand clasping hers and his voice desperate. "Zania means nothing to me. She was just some fun until you and I—"

"If you think there will *ever* be a 'you and I' now, then you can think again! Whatever feelings I had for you are long gone."

His grip tightened as he straightened, and she resisted crying out at his brute strength as he looked down at her and held her stare. "You've been panting after me for months. As a sheikha, surely you must realize that between your overzealous brother, your security team and your sheikh *friend* I've had to be patient and bide my time."

"If I'd known that meant sating yourself with my best friend while waiting for an appropriate time to date me, I wouldn't have looked at you twice!" Her lip curled at seeing the smeared lipstick up close and personal on his mouth. "You disgust me."

He sucked in a disbelieving breath. "You bitch," he snarled. "I haven't been waiting for you all this time just to have it ripped away from me for some silly little indiscretion."

His grip on her suddenly loosened, the hairs on the back of her neck prickling as Dhamar stood between them like some avenging angel, effortlessly separating her from Tabari. A roar filled her ears, intensifying as something far from improper surged through her at seeing his savage face, his raw vehemence.

He'd tear the world apart to defend the woman he loved. And suddenly, painfully, she was envious of whoever that woman might be.

Dhamar shoved the older man away from her. "Touch her again, Tabari, and you won't have any hands to do it a second time."

It wasn't an idle threat, and Tabari's demeanor immediately changed. He lifted a placating hand. "Sheikh Dhamar, I apologize. There really is no excuse for my behavior. But what I can't apologize for is my feelings for Aisha."

Her chest expanded as hope filled her veins and scorched through all her nausea and doubts. Did he really mean that?

Dhamar's breath hissed with patent disbelief. "And disrespect is how you show your feelings toward her?"

Tabari's gaze flickered. "You and I both know she has a way of pushing all the wrong buttons."

Aisha flinched, her eyes suddenly hot. Was she *that* maddening and provoking? Was that why he'd turned to Zania? She was demure, proper and discreet, everything Aisha was not.

Yeah, Zania was so discreet she managed to have an affair behind my back with the man of my dreams.

Pain sliced through Aisha. How could she ever trust anyone again?

She'd yearned with everything she'd had for Tabari to fall in love with her. That he'd barely shown interest in her, until now, was painfully obvious. Had it taken nearly losing her to open his eyes to what was right in front of him?

The thought gave her a rash of goose bumps, and Dhamar turned his frown her way and said, "You're cold."

When he took off his jacket and placed it over her shoulders, she unconsciously tucked it closer while breathing in its expensive scent that was mixed with his own unique mahogany and crisp oceanic scent.

He refocused on Tabari, his whole body stiff and unyielding. "In case you've forgotten, it's Aisha's birthday today—a day for celebration, not for cheating and aggression. Being that she pushes all your wrong buttons, I suggest that you leave."

Aisha gaped. What the hell was he doing? Tabari had been the very first name on her guest list.

"You're not serious," Tabari spluttered. "I was invited."

"And now I'm uninviting you," Dhamar said quietly, but with enough ruthless intent in his voice that Tabari took a backward step. "Leave this island now, or the debt you owe me will be brought to the forefront of my attention."

Tabari's face paled. "You're blackmailing me?" He shook his head. "You have more money than you know what to do with—"

"I'm a businessman, Tabari, not a charity. But I'm also a reasonable man. Find a way off this island within the hour and your debt is paid-in-full."

Aisha stepped forward, the coat wrapped around her barely taking away her sudden chill. "What? *No!*" She glowered at Dhamar. "You don't get to decide who stays or leaves my birthday party."

Dhamar's nostrils flared. "Believe it or not, it's for your own good."

Tabari's jaw clenched, his dark eyes glittering. "I see now what's going on. You set me up." His lips thinned, making him look older than his forty-six years. "You want her all for yourself!"

Aisha shook her head. "That isn't true, Tabari." She smiled at him, though a part of her looked at him through different lenses, ones a little more cynical and less...rosy. "This has all been a terrible misunderstanding. I'm sure—"

"Don't," Dhamar interjected quietly. She glanced at him, at the gleam of dark-gold in his troubled eyes. "Don't demean and lower yourself to his level. Not ever."

She blinked, suddenly unable to tear her eyes away from his. And just as powerless to talk. Why did he care so much?

Tabari threw his head back and laughed. "Oh, you're good, Dhamar." He sobered just as quickly. "I never stood a chance, did I?"

Dhamar directed a scathing look at the other man. "Your own actions saw to that."

"I was a fool," Tabari acknowledged. He exhaled heavily, then turned to Aisha. "For what it's worth, I'm sorry."

Aisha shook her head. "It doesn't have to be like this."

Tabari's smile was a twist of his lips. "But it does." He glanced meaningfully at Dhamar. "A certain someone saw to that." Looking back at her, Tabari took another step back. "Good luck, Aisha." His tone suggested she was going to need it. Then taking one last, lingering appraisal of her, he turned on his heel and he was gone.

Chapter Three

As Tabari walked away, Aisha saw any possible future relationship disappear right along with him. All her hopes and dreams gone. It didn't matter that the man was a rogue, it only mattered that it was *her* decision to tell him to go...or stay.

She rounded on Dhamar. "You had *no* right to tell Tabari to leave. *None!* He was *my* guest!"

Dhamar looked at her with a granite-hard expression. "You'd date a worthless cheater?"

"Who I choose to date is *my* business, not yours!"

She went to storm past, but he caught her by the elbow and turned her back around to face him. His dark golden eyes searched hers. "Be honest, Aisha. Were you thinking of Tabari when you were kissing me?"

She swallowed hard, unable to process any kind of defense past the sudden lump in her throat. It defied logic that she'd gotten lost in Dhamar's kiss, or that any and all thought had dissolved while her mouth had been plundered by his.

She lifted her chin, her voice turning frosty. "If I remember correctly, *you* kissed me. I was just too shocked to do anything about it."

"And yet if I kissed you again right now I bet you wouldn't fight it. You'd enjoy every second of it."

She glowered, clutching at straws when she gritted out, "My brother would throw you off this island if he knew you dared to kiss me."

Dhamar arched a brow. "Or perhaps he'd demand that we marry."

She almost stumbled back at the hunger his words induced, her mind conjuring up their naked bodies on their marital bed, their pent-up passion fueled by the too many unspoken words between them. She shook her head. He was seriously delusional! *She* was seriously delusional! "That won't ever happen!"

He kept a poker face. "Isn't marrying a sheikh every girls dream?"

She crossed her arms. "I'm not that shallow. I want to be with a man who makes my heart beat fast whenever I'm near him. A man who knows how to make me blush and makes me imagine a future together."

"Sounds like you're talking about us."

"*Ugh!* I don't know why I'm so shocked by your arrogance. But I am. Now, if you'll excuse me, I have my birthday—"

"Don't you want to know what I got you?"

She paused, intrigued despite herself. "You bought me a present?"

"Of course. I couldn't come here empty-handed."

Unlike Tabari. All she'd gotten from him was his betrayal with her best friend. Scalding, wet heat flooded her eyes. She blinked it away, doing her best to toughen up. But damn it, the love of her life and her one true friendship was now utterly, irreversibly broken.

It was almost too much to take in.

She was just grateful Dhamar was the perfect distraction.

"What is it?" she asked, her voice wobbly.

He reached into his inner jacket pocket and withdrew an envelope. Handing it to her, he said, "Happy birthday, princess."

She bit into her bottom lip, then opened the envelope, pressing a hand to her mouth at seeing the photograph of Black Zippy—the one and same Arabian filly she'd bid on and lost at auction against Dhamar—along with her receipt of ownership. "Are you serious?" she gasped.

"I am. She's all yours now." He smiled at her delight. "I put my best horse trainer to work on her. She's ready now for you to ride without fear of getting thrown off."

Aisha was a competent horse rider, but even she wouldn't have dared to ride the headstrong and fiery black filly. The young horse had played up even as she'd been led into the auction yard under halter, where bids had quickly escalated for the filly with her illustrious endurance bloodline.

Overcome by emotion, Aisha threw herself at Dhamar, clinging onto his strong body as exhilaration soon became something else entirely...something self-aware and entirely too sensual. It could have been seconds but was likely long, slow minutes before she peeled herself from him, her face flushed and her breathing erratic. "I'm sorry."

He shook his head. "Don't apologize, princess. I kind of liked it." His eyes glinted as he confessed starkly, "I *more* than liked it."

Her face warmed further, while other, intimate parts of her body radiated heat. What the hell was happening to her? She didn't even like the man. They rubbed each other the wrong way, always had. She routinely spent way too much time thinking about him and his downfall.

She cleared her throat and lifted the envelope with its contents threatening to spill onto the ground. "Thank you for my gift. I can't wait to ride her."

He nodded and smiled. "You're more than welcome to visit any time, day or night."

She frowned, her joy slipping. "Wait—what? You're not sending her to my brother's palace stables?"

Dhamar cocked his head to the side. "My palace is close to the foothills of some of the most amazing riding trails in all of the Middle East. You would get much more enjoyment riding her there."

She resisted stamping her foot. He really was insufferable. "As if my brother would ever allow me to go off to your country alone!"

"What makes you think I haven't already discussed the idea with him?"

"Hamid would never agree!"

"Did I hear my name?"

She twisted around to see her brother and his wife, Holly, walking toward them hand-in-hand. "Hamid, what are you doing here?" she said weakly.

Holly had a knowing grin on her face while Hamid seemed unaware of the tension running between his sister and Dhamar.

Her brother arched a dark brow. "What do you mean what am I doing here? It's my baby sister's birthday and you were nowhere to be found. And it seems your security team was too lax to make sure you were safe."

"That was my fault," Dhamar admitted. "I knew she'd be safe with me and asked them to give her a bit of space."

Hamid's eyes narrowed speculatively. "Their job isn't to trust others with her welfare. Their job is to keep her safe at all costs. I pay them well to do just that."

Holly put a hand on her husband's shoulder. "I know you mean well, Hamid, but she's on an island surrounded by water, and with someone you trust. I bet she was just as relieved for some privacy as I am whenever I get some time alone."

Hamid nodded, his shoulders loosening beneath his traditional thobe. "You're right, little flame." He turned back to Aisha with a smile. "Just as long as you're never alone with Tabari, I promise I won't go too OTT big brother on you."

Aisha's throat closed up. Had she been the only one blinded by Tabari's charm?

You mean other than your best friend, Zania?

"You don't have to worry about Tabari anymore," Aisha gritted out. "Dhamar sent him off the island."

Hamid smirked. "Really?" He cleared his throat and managed to rein in his delight. "I'm guessing from the conversation I overheard you've finally seen Dhamar's present?"

She exhaled long and slow. "I have." She looked at Dhamar with a little glare even as she conceded, "I'm grateful, I truly am."

"But?" Hamid prompted.

"But Black Zippy is staying at Dhamar's palace stables."

Her brother tilted his head to the side. "And that bothers you?"

"Of course it bothers me! When will I ever be allowed to go off by myself to ride a horse that isn't even in my own country?"

"You're twenty years old," Hamid said with a wistful smile. "You're no longer a baby. I trust Dhamar to keep you safe if—*when*—you go over there."

Aisha blinked. "But that goes against everything you've ever—"

"Just thank your brother and be happy." Dhamar glanced at Hamid and Holly, and added, "I remember how much she wanted Black Zippy two years ago at auction. Now the filly is almost a mare and is a quiet and reliable mount I'd trust just about anyone to ride."

Hamid nodded. "You don't have to reassure me, I know you'll do everything in your power to see she isn't hurt." He grimaced. "And I can honestly say she never did like riding my camels half as much as she did my horses."

Dhamar laughed. "I feel the same way. Give me a horse any day over those wretched humped animals."

Holly giggled. "Now you're stepping on my husband's toes. You know how much he adores his camels."

Hamid's plaits slid forward as he nodded. "Without them I wouldn't have been able to explore half the desert."

"Not to mention, without them you would never have stumbled across me and saved my life."

"My camels are worth their weight in gold," Hamid said softly, but with enough somberness to enforce his gratitude to his beasts.

Aisha sighed heavily. She was happy for her brother, she really was, but it didn't stop a pang of envy knowing she'd no longer find that same level of love and faith with Tabari. She feigned a yawn. "As much as I've enjoyed my birthday, I'm honestly really tired right now."

"Too tired to cut your own birthday cake?" Holly asked.

Aisha grimaced. It would look beyond churlish if she went to bed early. Managing a smile, she said, "I'd forgotten about my cake. I guess I'd better get back to the celebrations."

As Hamid and Holly murmured agreement, then turned and retraced their steps, Dhamar leaned close and said, "Allow me to escort you back to your party."

Though a part of her wanted to tell him to go fuck himself, a bigger part of her leaned in close and accepted his proffered arm. He might rub her the wrong way at all times, but she...trusted him.

She silently gulped. *Holy crap.* Out of all the men in her life, Dhamar was one of the few she really *did* trust. It was nothing short of a revelation. Yes, he'd kissed her, but she had no doubt he could have taken that kiss a whole lot further.

She'd been lost to him.

Little wonder her brother trusted him.

She was deep in thought when they returned to where the birthday function was officially being held, and it was rather gratifying then to find Zania all alone near the bar and dancefloor, her so called best friend's expression caught somewhere between guilt and confusion, before her dark eyes widened at seeing Aisha with Dhamar.

It somehow gave her the strength and confidence to sail past Zania to where the table held the three tier cake with its white and pink frosting, with the piped words *Happy Birthday, Aisha.*

It wasn't traditional to have candles on a cake or to blow them out, indeed it was frowned upon by many of her people, but it'd become something of a custom to cut a birthday cake and share slices of it around to guests.

Her brother had the music stopped, and all the guests turned her way and smiled expectantly at her. She smiled back, ever the consummate sheikha. "I want to thank you all for coming to my birthday party. As you know the celebrations will be a week-long event, and I sincerely hope you can all stay for the duration and enjoy this lovely island with me."

Unlike Tabari.

Her eyes locked onto Dhamar, the one and same man who'd gotten rid of Tabari without her consent. He smiled back, his dark eyes glinting. Her hands fisted at his audacity. She'd been in love with Tabari for what seemed like forever, had dreamed of marrying him some day!

Dhamar had effectively squashed that dream as effectively as he'd squashed Tabari's presence here. Like her dreams and her desires meant nothing to him.

That he was looking at her like she was now *his* biggest desire shouldn't make her face flush and her stomach pull in all directions. He wanted what he couldn't have. He must be getting bored of all those insipid, beautiful women who fell at his feet.

The knowledge didn't reverse her feelings toward him. Not one bit. He might be as handsome as sin, but she'd forever despise him.

He was powerful enough to manipulate people like puppets, just like he'd manipulated Tabari. That Dhamar had some kind of financial hold over the older man didn't surprise her. Dhamar was a living, breathing bank account who even put her brother and every other wealthy sheikh on the planet in the shade.

Not even the newly appointed Sheikh of Dumak, Sheikh Kain Al Hadi, who had recently stepped up to his duty and position of power after his father passed, was as obscenely wealthy. Her eyes narrowed as that same sheikh approached Zania. It seemed her friend really was attracting quite the male interest of late.

Someone in the crowd cleared his throat at Aisha's silence, and she turned away from Zania and Sheikh Kain, and pasted on a brighter smile. "In the meantime, who wants cake?"

Everyone clapped and a staff member hurried forward with a shiny cake knife, its handle wrapped in a pretty pink ribbon.

"Let me help you with that."

She started at Dhamar's voice. That he was right next to her made her whole body tremble with both responsiveness and rejection. She lifted her chin and said in a furious undertone, "I'm quite sure I can cut the cake all by myself."

"I'm sure you can, too," he said with a somberness that belied a self-assured smile. "But you might look bad-mannered if I leave you now to cut it alone."

She looked back at the guests, at their heightened state of anticipation at seeing him standing so close to her. It had become something of a tradition in her circle of family and friends to have someone help cut the birthday cake once they'd reached an appropriate age.

"Fine," she said through gritted teeth. When his hand closed over hers on the handle of the knife, she managed to ignore the sparks of heat that ran up her arm before settling in the very core of her. What she couldn't ignore were the bright flashes of cameras that bore witness to the event.

Damn it! They weren't a couple, they never would be!

The knife blade slid through the top tier of the cake before she released it to Dhamar's capable grasp and turned to the guests. "I hope you'll all join me in thanking Dhamar for filling in for Tabari, who unfortunately couldn't be here tonight to help me cut my birthday cake."

A scattering of applause broke out as Aisha stepped back so that the same staff member who brought the knife could cut the rest of the cake. The guests made their way forward to sample a slice of cake made by a renowned cake maker.

Yet as Aisha walked away, she'd never been more self-conscious and aware of a man's gaze on her. A shiver slid through her. She couldn't shake the feeling Dhamar would find swift retribution thanks to her little speech.

Chapter Four

Dhamar watched Aisha sashay away like the regal princess he wanted to make her. Whether she wanted that too was beside the point. She'd been infatuated with the wrong man for too long already and he didn't regret opening her eyes to Tabari's true nature.

She was far too good for the man.

That she blamed Dhamar and hated him even more now was something he intended to change fast. She'd enjoyed his kiss, had responded to him like a spark to fuel. His cock kicked at the reminder and he gritted his teeth to ignore the sexual urge he'd repressed for too long already.

Instructing the staff to save some leftover cake for Aisha, he left them to distribute it to the partygoers and hurried after Aisha. But not before he glanced at her brother, Hamid, who nodded support. His desire to bring Dhamar into the family was all too apparent.

Dhamar knew better than to imagine it was his money Hamid wanted. All Hamid cared about was getting his sister away from Tabari and finding a man who genuinely cared about her. And it was patently clear to everyone but Aisha that Dhamar cared about her...more than cared about her.

She was halfway to her holiday apartment when he caught up to her, the solar lights casting just enough light to make the scene romantic. "Aisha, wait."

She flung around to face him, her liquid dark eyes flashing. *Huh.* This was clearly no romance scene. "What do you want now? Haven't you done enough damage for one night?"

Despite her dark mood, he'd be blind not to notice how attracted she was to him. But then there had always been a powerful chemistry between them, no matter how much she might deny it. Satisfaction poured through his veins, a smile curling his lips. "I think it's pretty obvious what I want. And you were fortunate that I stopped any damage that might have been done if I hadn't stepped in."

"You don't get it, do you?" she snapped. "I want to be with Tabari. He's all I've ever thought about these past four years. He's the only man I've ever wanted and he's—"

Dhamar stepped forward and sealed his lips over hers. Partly because he couldn't stand to hear the other man's name ever again, and partly because he needed to remind her how little she really wanted Tabari—the supposed love of her life—when Dhamar was kissing her.

She softened for a moment before she jerked her head back, her breaths erratic and her face flushed. "Are you *trying* to make an enemy out of my brother? If he caught you kissing me he'd—"

"Probably shake my hand and congratulate me for distracting you from the letch you imagine you're in love with."

She crossed her arms, her lip curling in contempt. "The real problem is that you've always managed to buy people off."

"Like I did with Tabari?" he mused aloud.

She stiffened. "Yes, like you did with Tabari."

That she was still hurt that Dhamar had gotten rid of the man who'd done the dirty on her made him want to shake some sense into her. "Someone had to open your eyes."

"And that someone just had to be *you,* right?"

"It's only lucky I'm strong enough to take the fallout that comes with being your scapegoat."

Her bottom lip quivered, until all he wanted was to kiss her again and turn her outrage into desire, making her whole body tremble with a far healthier emotion.

"You arrogant—"

"Aisha, can we talk?"

Dhamar turned simultaneously with Aisha to see her best friend, Zania, approach them.

"Talk?" Aisha repeated in a shrill voice.

Zania blinked. "Have I caught you at a bad time?" She looked between them, the gears in her brain clearly whirring. Had she seen them kiss? Dhamar almost hoped she had.

Aisha raised her voice a little more, its sharpness all too clear. "Since when did you care enough to worry about anyone but yourself?"

Zania's face dropped, her eyes flashing with remorse. "So you know, then."

"No thanks to you or Tabari, yes, I *do* know."

"You have to believe I never meant for any of it to happen, I was just swept away in the moment, believing all Tabari's promises...his lies."

"You're my best friend!" Aisha refuted hotly. "How could you?"

"It looks as though you were both fooled by the man." Dhamar was selfish enough to be relieved it'd been Zania who'd been completely played, not Aisha. Because then Aisha might well have been forced to marry the man, playing right into his filthy hands.

Dhamar grimaced. *No.* He wouldn't have allowed that to happen, not even if she'd lost her virginity to the older man. Dhamar would have appealed to her brother, made Hamid realize it was in everyone's best interests that Aisha marry him, not the sleazy Tabari.

"And I bet you're happy!" Aisha snapped at him. "Not only can't he defend himself since you sent him off the island, you have free rein to say whatever you like about him and expect us to believe you over him."

"H-he's gone?" Zania asked, her voice stricken and her face pale.

Aisha glared at her friend. "He is. Feel free to follow him off the island."

With that she spun on her heel, her dark hair flying around her like some beautiful pagan witch of old. She marched away and Dhamar's pulse quickened. Damn, she was glorious!

Zania took a backward step, her hands clenched by her sides. "I should have known *you* would be the only one of us to get the person you want," she choked out.

He nodded, not even a little bit abashed. "I knew sooner or later Tabari would reveal his true self to Aisha. It's just unfortunate that revelation happened while he was making out with her best friend."

Zania gasped, her eyes flooding with tears as the truth dawned. "She didn't just stumble across us, did she? You brought her to my apartment when I was with Tabari."

"Don't act so shocked. You were making out with him outside of your apartment in public where anyone could have seen. You both deserved to be caught."

She shook her head, her eyes wide. "You've been in lust with Aisha for four long years, biding your time and waiting patiently to gain her trust. It mattered little who got hurt along the way."

He narrowed his eyes at her. "I didn't hurt anyone. You did that all on your own. *You* broke her trust, not me."

"And now you'll take care of her while she's at her most vulnerable, right?"

"I'll *always* be there for her, I always have. That will never change."

Envy lit up Zania's eyes, bright spots of color on her cheeks. "It must be nice to be so loved!"

He watched as Zania stormed off, a twinge of pity contracting his stomach for the woman who'd no doubt fallen for Tabari's empty promises. Dhamar had no idea if Aisha would keep Zania on staff after her betrayal, either way he'd have someone keep an eye on the woman. Jealousy was a dangerous, toxic emotion.

You should know.

He ignored the snide little voice. He'd protect Aisha with his life. She'd be his. She just didn't know it yet.

Chapter Five

Aisha woke to midday sunlight blazing against her eyelids and sweet-morphing-into-pesky birdsong filling her ears.

She rolled over, unwilling yet to face the world. Not when she'd spent half the night tossing and turning, and the rest of the night having vivid dreams about Dhamar. That the dreams had been sexual in nature and had left her hot and bothered only made her more irritable.

She hadn't once dreamed about Tabari!

Had his and Zania's betrayal cut too deep to examine too closely, even in her dreams? *Or is Dhamar's pursuit of you making you see him in a new, far more sexual light?*

How was it possible to both hate and lust a person in equal measure?

Of course she'd always noticed his tall, lean body, his corded shoulders and narrow waist, his dark honey eyes and the three day stubble that leant him a dangerous air. His tailor-made suits and clothes that screamed power and money only added to his magnetism, his authority.

But she'd never wanted him...never wanted to be another woman in his long line of lovers. She'd been determined to be special, loved. She wanted someone of Tabari's maturity to value her as more than just a pretty face...more than a sheikha.

She shuddered and pushed her fingertips against her forehead as a headache threatened. Too bad Tabari had valued Aisha's best friend as the perfect replacement fuck until Aisha had been ready to go to the next level in their "relationship."

She bit into her bottom lip. Had she seriously been that naïve? Of course someone of Tabari's experience didn't want to wait around for her to make herself available to him. He was a virile man, sex was no doubt an integral part of his life.

That Dhamar had chased him off the island—on her birthday no less!—was infuriating and despicable. She'd had such grand plans. Had imagined all kinds of romantic and sexy scenarios with Tabari.

Like having sex with him? Too bad Zania had had that same idea.

Aisha threw aside her covers and climbed out of bed. She needed to use the bathroom. And she needed a shower. She couldn't function without first washing her hair and sluicing hot water over her now chilled body.

It wasn't until she'd finished in the bathroom and was lost in thought while towel-drying her hair in the sitting room that she noticed the time on the wall clock. She'd been meant to meet her family and guests at the island's main restaurant for lunch. She was already half-an-hour late.

She was only surprised her brother hadn't gotten one of her many bodyguards—one of whom always discreetly watched her apartment—to bang on her door and check up on her.

Knock. Knock.

"Surprise, surprise," she muttered under her breath, before swinging open the front door.

Her heart stuttered and she gulped as she stared up at the dark-haired man who'd fulfilled fantasies she hadn't even known she had, until last night. Her eyes narrowed as she forced herself to remember other, far more unpleasant memories...real ones where he'd acted on her behalf without her permission. "Dhamar. What do you want?"

Her distinctly unfriendly tone didn't seem to affect him. He smiled lazily, his stare moving slowly up and down her little floral nightgown she'd belted around her naked body. When she realized her breasts were half-showing, warmth tingled straight to her core as her nipples tightened like over-ripened buds.

"Do you always open the door half-dressed?" he murmured silkily.

"Only to people I really like. If I'd known it was you I would have thrown on a burqa." At the amused glint in his eyes, she tossed back her stringy, wet hair. She probably looked like a half-drowned rat. "Are you going to tell me what you want?"

"I'm afraid what I want is irrelevant right now."

Going by the lump in his pants and the feral gleam in his eyes she was no half-drowned rat and he, too, wanted what she'd dreamed about last night. Too bad neither of them would ever fulfill that particular fantasy.

Fantasy? Her pulse accelerated as denial swept through her. More like a nightmare.

He cleared his throat and added huskily, "Your brother and the rest of your guests are waiting for the birthday girl to show up."

"My birthday was yesterday," she reminded him. "And being that I'm twenty now, I'm really not a girl anymore."

"True," he said. "You're all woman now."

She forced a smile, though every nerve ending tingled at his words, at his patent appreciation. *Ugh,* she couldn't deal with this...with these crazy, mixed up emotions and signals she no longer knew how to read. "Please tell my brother and guests I'll be there in ten minutes."

She went to shut the door when he stuck his foot in the gap, then pushed the door wide open again. "I promised your brother I'd escort you safely to lunch."

She folded her arms across her chest. "Oh? And does my brother have *any* idea of what you really want to do with me?"

"He's not a fool." He shrugged his shoulders. "But he trusts me as much as I trust him, and that means everything to the both of us."

She narrowed her eyes, forcing back a whole lot of disparaging words before she said grudgingly, "Then I suppose you'd better wait in my sitting room."

"I'll do that." He smirked. "Thank you for the invitation."

She glared after his retreating back as he stalked through her spacious apartment and into its sitting room, where fiction books were set into built-in shelves and comfortable chairs looked out toward big bay windows to the beach and ocean beyond. Yet all she noticed was his physique and his superbly fitted navy-blue slacks and his blue and white pinstriped polo.

She adored his western clothes. She only wished she had the same options.

Her wardrobe was made up almost entirely of Middle Eastern clothes, with abayas and hijabs her key garments. That the fabrics were beautiful and soft, and in various colors, with her formal ones studded with gorgeous gems, didn't make her feel any less resentful. She was a woman, and therefore she had to obey the dictates of what was considered respectable fashion.

It must have driven her brother crazy on those few occasions when she'd worn the harem costumes that'd been left behind after Holly had come into his life. Luckily Holly had enjoyed dressing up in them too, with the sole intention of getting Hamid hot and bothered.

It had clearly worked. Then again, Holly could have worn a burlap sack and Aisha's brother would have still wanted her. Aisha sighed heavily. How must it feel to be a commoner and know that having a sheikha title wasn't what drew men in like flies?

She turned her back on her nemesis. She needed to get dressed.

Fifteen minutes later she was standing in front of her bedroom mirror, her long damp hair caught up in a messy bun, and a sequined belt caught around her loose flowing aqua abaya, changing it from shapeless and into something closer to an evening gown. Adding sparkling strappy shoes and earrings, she suddenly felt a whole lot better about the day ahead.

Like she'd been able to make a choice that was hers alone, and she wasn't completely and utterly helpless.

Lining kohl under her eyes and spraying some light, violet-scented perfume on her wrists and behind her ears, she padded quietly into the sitting room. Dhamar was reclined on a padded seat, resting his ankle on his opposite knee as he stared broodingly out the window to the magnificent views.

"Ready when you are."

He turned in his chair, his eyes appraising her and seemingly finding approval even before he said, "So beautiful."

"And I'm sure you know you're every bit as handsome."

"Handsome?" he repeated with a slow smile spreading over his face.

She nodded, annoyed by her choice of words that he'd spun in a positive light. "In your own way."

His smile only broadened. "As in not gray and wrinkled and past my prime?" He coughed to hold back a spluttering laugh. "That just might be the nicest thing you've ever said to me."

She resisted stamping a foot and letting loose with a string of unladylike obscenities. That he'd been speaking of Tabari made her blood boil. Instead she smiled right back at him and said in her sweetest voice, "We better not keep everyone waiting."

He uncoiled his long, sinewy body and pushed to his feet, and even in her heels she was dwarfed by him. Why couldn't she have the height of a model? She wasn't diminutive like Zania, but he certainly made her feel that way. That she needed to wrest every advantage against this man was an understatement.

It was only once she'd shut the front door behind her and they were walking along the pathway, where tropical breezes carried the usual heady aromas of sea-salt and frangipani, that she asked, "What would my brother say if he knew you were in my apartment alone with me?"

"Maybe he thought you'd be dressed in that burqa you reserve for people like me?" He nodded behind them, where a bodyguard trailed discreetly. "And just remember, you're never truly alone, princess."

She sniffed. "My bodyguard is supposed to keep me safe from possible intruders. I find it odd that you can simply knock on my door and step inside as though you're a welcomed and trustworthy guest."

"Are you saying that I'm not?"

She huffed out a breath. "I'm saying that you seem to be allowed to break a whole lot of rules in regards to your friendship with me."

"Is that how you see me? As a friend?"

"That's putting it politely. Nemesis is usually the word that springs to mind."

He laughed then, a deep baritone sound that sent shivers down her spine before spreading once again into an area far too intimate for her peace of mind. He held her gaze, his honey-gold eyes glinting. "I'm glad that I leave such a distinct impression."

There was nothing more she could say to that, and she kept silent as they walked up some railed, wide concrete stairs and through frosted-glass, automated doors that slid open into the large restaurant. The scent of cooked meat, onion and seafood assailed her and she inhaled deeply as they skirted tables where her guests were already waiting. She managed to smile at most of them as she and Dhamar approached the far table where her brother Hamid sat with his wife Holly.

Only when Holly saw them did she stand up, lift the camera dangling around her neck, and snap a couple of pictures.

Aisha frowned. There was no way Dhamar would allow photos. Then he slid an arm around her waist and drew her closer to him, and murmured, "Smile, princess."

She stiffened. "You *want* a photo of us together?"

He was an intensely private man. Most sheikhs were, for good reason. A picture might speak a thousand words, but it could also be misconstrued in a thousand different ways.

"Why not?"

Holly grinned at them, her flame-red hair a dramatic foil for the emerald green of her frock. "I've already discussed it with Dhamar. If you are happy for me to sell the photo, all the proceeds will go to your charity."

Aisha's mind whirred. Dhamar had agreed to...this? That made about as much sense as Holly selling the photos without making a profit. Then again, her sister-in-law didn't need the income, far from it, and the exposure alone would step her up another rung on the ladder of being one of the most sought after photographers in the country, if she wasn't already.

That she was a woman photographer made it an even bigger deal.

And Aisha couldn't deny that her charity, which helped educate underprivileged women, would benefit hugely from the money.

Holly's smile gentled. "It would fetch a huge amount to the right buyer."

Aisha nodded. "Fine." She glanced at Dhamar, whose arm was still draped around her waist. "As long as you're fine with that."

He looked down at her. "Of course. It's all in a good cause."

Is that why he looked like the cat that ate the canary?

After Holly took a couple more shots, Dhamar released his hold on Aisha and pulled out a chair at the head of the table, which had been reserved solely for her use thanks to it being her birthday. Her legs suddenly shaky, she was relieved to sit down. Dhamar took the chair to her right, and for the first time she noticed Zania, who was already seated next to him. Her brother sat opposite Dhamar and to Aisha's left, Holly sat next to Hamid and opposite Zania.

That Sheikh Kain Al Hadi sat on Zania's other side was suddenly all too noticeable. As Aisha's best friend, Zania had long enjoyed certain privileges, like sitting with royalty. But Aisha couldn't help but question it all now in a fit of spite. Her best friend had done the dirty on her! She had no right to be here let alone sitting beside and flirting with one of the most eligible bachelors on the island.

It could be worse. She could be flirting with Dhamar instead.

Aisha's whole body stiffened, a slow burn working its way to her stomach. Then she shook off her silly fabrication and refocused on the people at her table.

Nine more guests sat farther along, all VIPs she didn't know that well. She would have preferred Hamid's best friends and their wives, who were fast becoming her friends, too, but most were preoccupied with their growing families.

She sniffed. She hadn't minded them being MIA, not when she'd imagined having Tabari seated by her side, where Dhamar sat instead. That Zania would have been in her element by also being next to Tabari made Aisha's blood boil yet again.

It took everything she had simply to regain her composure and distract herself by looking around the rest of the room. Bodyguards were sprinkled throughout the dining area, standing watch with stern expressions. Diners seated at the other tables were no doubt impatient and hungry by her lateness.

The wait-staff emerged through the kitchen swinging doors to bring out the first course and the guests began chatting amongst themselves again. It made Aisha realize all eyes had been on her and Dhamar, with barely a word exchanged by anyone else the entire time.

Then she heard her and Dhamar's name in the same sentence in conversations around them, and anxiety stirred deep inside. She didn't like that the guests were beginning to believe she and Dhamar were an item...a couple.

Sending off Tabari had only accelerated that conclusion.

How convenient!

Hamid leaned close to Dhamar and said, "I hear your ballroom is close to finished."

Dhamar nodded. "You heard right."

Aisha scowled. Wasn't the ballroom a bet her brother had made with three of his best friends, which stated when one of them fell in love they had to build and make use of the ballroom with the love of their life for any future events?

So why had Dhamar felt the need to build one, too? Yes, he was becoming a close friend of Hamid's, but he hadn't been included in the bet at the time. What was he trying to prove?

She flicked back a strand of hair that had fallen free from her upsweep. What did it matter? She should be focused on the fact Dhamar had chased off her love interest before making moves on her while secretly being in love with some other woman.

Her stomach twisted. Could any man be trusted?

Clearly not. That Dhamar *was* usually the trustworthy one made her skin burn, queasiness filling her.

"Aren't you hungry?" Dhamar asked her in a proprietorial tone.

She looked down at her first course. Roast duck breast with truffles and fragrant rice. It could have been cardboard. "Not really."

He cut a piece of her duck and pronged it onto his fork, then lifted it to her lips. "Try it. I promise you'll love it."

She should tell him to go to hell, or at the very least go back to the woman he loved. But there was now a breathless silence in the room, with every eye in the restaurant on them once again. Forcing a regal smile, she opened her mouth and closed it over the prongs, withdrawing the juicy piece of duck before chewing.

"Good isn't it?" Dhamar asked, using his fork then to pierce a piece of his own duck before closing his mouth over it.

She shivered, transfixed by his lips that were on the same tines hers had been. How could such a simple act be so...erotic? She cleared her throat. "It's good," she conceded. To prove her point she ate a little more, only to find she was, indeed, hungry. All too soon she'd cleared her plate and was waiting impatiently for the next course to come out.

"You always did have a good appetite," Hamid said approvingly.

Aisha arched a brow. "You once told me I had an appetite for trouble."

"Just the once?" Hamid replied with a chuckle. "I mean, how often did you lead Zania into strife?"

Aisha's gaze clashed with the other woman's before she said icily, "Turns out Zania finds strife just fine all on her own."

Zania flushed and Hamid frowned. "Is something going on I don't know about?"

Zania looked down at her food. Had no one noticed *she* hadn't eaten one bite? Then Kain leaned close and whispered something into her ear. Clearly *he'd* noticed. He only had eyes for her.

Dhamar shook his head. "I think it's fair to say Zania is yet another victim of a smooth talking man who used his experience to—"

"Victim?" Aisha cut in, voice high-pitched. "You're kidding me, right?"

Dhamar sighed heavily. "You're obviously still seeing Tabari as an innocent man, not someone who tried to take advantage of two young, impressionable women."

"All I'm seeing is my best friend who cheated with the man she knew I was crazy about!"

Hamid's frown deepened. "I'd say your best friend did you a favor."

Aisha glared at Zania, and though her eyes were downcast she was visibly upset. Guilt pricked Aisha's conscience, which was immediately overridden by anger. Why was she feeling bad? She wasn't in the wrong!

She pushed her chair back, its legs scraping loudly. "I can't sit here and take any more of this!"

Except suddenly Dhamar's hand clamped around her wrist, stopping her from going anywhere as he spoke to her in an undertone. "Do you want this broadcast all over the country tomorrow? Sit down and behave, princess. I know you're hurt, but there is a time and place for this."

Chapter Six

Dhamar hated acting the dictator, but there was no way he'd see Aisha's name splashed all over the papers for all the wrong reasons. She didn't deserve that kind of infamy.

There was a breathless kind of hush around the table, around the entire restaurant, then Aisha sank back onto her seat with a poise that was remarkable for someone who was about ready to implode.

Hamid leaned forward, his dark eyes searching his sister's. "This isn't the kind of party I wanted for you, Aisha. We're all here to celebrate your birthday, not for you to be miserable."

Her eyes flashed, and she leaned forward to mutter to her brother, "Then does it matter to you that Dhamar sent away the one guest I wanted here?"

Hamid shook his head. "Why can everyone see what an absolute letch Tabari is—except you," he glanced at Zania, "and your friend?" He sighed heavily. "I should have put my foot down a long time ago about him, but I thought your good sense would overcome any infatuation."

"Infatuation? Is that what you think this is?"

"You're still so young," Hamid said quietly. "Perhaps too young—"

"You were running the country at my age!" she burst out. Then lifting her chin she said, "I'm sorry I ruined your birthday plans for me, Hamid, I really am. But I'm not happy here. I-I just want to go home."

"Home?" Hamid stared at his sister like she'd grown another head. "And return to the man who no doubt hopes to console you? I don't think so!"

"Anywhere but here then!" she stated, her voice quivering.

Dhamar wanted to be the one to reach out to comfort and console her but he knew better. She blamed him for her misery and his touch would only make her hate him more. It didn't mean he wouldn't do whatever it took to change her mind about him.

Hamid glanced meaningfully at Dhamar. He nodded. He'd already discussed taking Aisha to his country, where she could get away from Tabari and open her eyes to other...possibilities. Riding the filly he'd bought as her birthday present had just been an excuse to get her there.

Either way, he was happy to bring forward their plans and make her see what a real man was willing to do for the woman he loved. That Hamid knew of Dhamar's feelings for his sister and Dhamar's intention to marry her was the only reason Hamid considered stretching their unwritten and strict rules about women—sheikhas in particular—to breaking point.

"Fine," Hamid assented, even as Holly looked between her husband and Dhamar with a faint frown. "If that is what you wish, Aisha, I won't force you to stay here."

"Thank you," Aisha said demurely, as if her outburst had never been.

"I have my personal jet here," Dhamar said smoothly. "There is no need to use your brother's aircraft."

Aisha shook her head. "That's not necessary—"

Hamid smiled. "Actually, if you want to leave tonight, then Dhamar's jet *is* your only option. My aircraft aren't due back until the end of the week."

"You can't order them here earlier?" she asked in a small, disbelieving voice.

"Not unless you expect planned maintenance to be just pushed aside along with the safety of every guest here."

"Fine." She looked at Dhamar, her dark, kohl-lined eyes blank of emotion. "If it's not too much trouble, I really would like to get out of here."

He nodded. "Nothing is ever too much trouble for you, princess." Dabbing his mouth with a napkin, he stood, then pulled out her chair. "We'd best get packing."

Aisha blinked. "You don't need to leave, I'm quite capable of—"

"On the contrary, I *do* need to leave too. There is nothing keeping me here now."

Zania's mouth went slack even as her eyes widened as her gaze swung between the two of them. She must be bursting to know what exactly was going on, but she knew better than to ask. She'd broken all trust with her best friend and he had doubts Aisha would ever forgive her.

He proffered his arm to Aisha and murmured solicitously, "Let's go, princess."

When she took it once again, he smiled. He didn't doubt for a second that it was all for appearances sake. She was into him, she just didn't realize it yet.

Less than three hours later they were in the sky. Dhamar leaned back in one of the many cream leather seats, sipping an aged whiskey and scarcely able to believe his good luck. Patience really was a virtue! He'd been waiting for this day for what seemed like forever.

Trying to woo a woman who was in love with another man had never sat well with him. But neither had seeing the woman he adored being taken advantage of. Tabari wanted marry into wealth and royalty, it was his one and only objective. Little wonder. Dhamar knew for a fact that Tabari's debts far outweighed his wealth. Aisha had been his ticket out of looming poverty.

Dhamar frowned. He couldn't believe Aisha had fallen for the crafty, older man. But then she'd led a sheltered life. She might have the same dad as Hamid but they had far different mothers. While Hamid's mom had died giving birth to him, Aisha had been born many years later thanks to one of her dad's mistresses.

That same woman had been paid off and lived far away, and Aisha had been raised by nannies, the same as Hamid. Dhamar was only surprised she'd turned out so fun-loving and adventurous, like she wanted to grab life by the throat and drag every moment from it.

He often wondered if her fixation with Tabari was from her need for a father figure in her life. It was common knowledge the old sheikh had become an empty shell after the death of his eldest son in a helicopter crash. His second-eldest son and his daughter had been of no real interest to him. The moment Aisha's father had paid out her mother, any regard for his only daughter had become negligible.

Hamid had been her only rock in a turbulent life. And even that rock had become shaky at times thanks to her brother's drinking problem.

"Where exactly are we going?" Aisha asked.

It was the first words she'd spoken since the restaurant. Even the offer of food and beverage while they were in the air had been answered by a curt shake of her head. That she deigned to look away from the window she'd been staring out of to finally make eye contact with him was a bonus.

He held her stare. "I thought you might like to see your birthday present from me."

Her eyes widened. "You're taking me to *your* country?" At his nod she said in an incredulous voice, "Despite what you might think, Hamid would never allow me there unchaperoned."

"Your brother knows I have your best interests at heart."

"Hah. The only interest you have is self-interest. I mean, what exactly are you going to tell your lady friend I'm doing there?"

He frowned. "Lady friend?"

"Yes." She tossed her head back. "The one you built the ballroom for. You have some nerve, don't you? Running off my love interest while your own lover is stashed away in your palace of wherever the hell you left her."

He almost snorted. Aisha clearly had no idea how much he adored her—*only* her. It might have been amusing if it wasn't so disappointing. "I'm surprised you don't also accuse me of having this woman locked away in one of my many dungeons."

"Are you saying she is?"

"Whoever I loved would never stay in some dank, dark dungeon. Not unless she asked really nicely."

Aisha glowered. "Let me guess...that is one of your many sexual proclivities."

His dick grew uncomfortably tight as images of what he'd like to do to Aisha in said dungeon went through his mind. "What would you know of my proclivities?" he asked.

Her face flamed. "I know nothing, and that is how I intend for it to stay."

We shall see, princess. We shall see. It took everything he had to keep his thoughts to himself.

Chapter Seven

If Aisha had thought her brother's security was over-the-top then Dhamar's team was a whole new level of crazy. She counted eleven big black SUV's coming toward them as Dhamar's jet taxied along his private airstrip.

Armed men in white thobes stepped out of the vehicles, their expressions stern and their hawk-like attention on their surroundings making her heart pitter-patter with sudden anxiety. She looked at Dhamar. "Is all this necessary?"

He nodded. "I promised your brother I'd keep you safe, I intend to honor that."

Then he took hold of her hand and drew her with him along the jet's walkway and down the steps that led onto the tarmac. The sun cast shadows as it slowly disappeared behind the horizon, but the heat still hit her in the face, the desert surrounding the tarmac making her feel about as insignificant as an ant in a field.

"Where are we?" she asked, squinting into the vast nothingness.

Dhamar grinned. "Don't panic, princess, my palace is a short ten minutes' drive from here."

One of the guards opened the back passenger door to the middle car and Dhamar nodded for her to climb in before he followed her, sliding across the back seat with its soft, luxurious leather, before the guard shut the door with a *clunk* behind them.

With military precision the men then climbed into the SUV's front and back of them and the whole procession moved forward. She sunk back onto the seat, feeling suddenly weary. Then Dhamar's strong arm moved around her and he drew her close, her head pillowed by his shoulder.

"Sleep princess, I'll take care of you."

Why did his words reassure her? She should hate him! She'd known from the moment she'd done her birthday speech that he'd find some form of retribution. What better way of doing just that than whisking her away to his own country, then keeping her as his guest and as far away from Tabari as possible?

It didn't seem to stop her from snuggling closer to him while her eyes drifted shut and she sank into darkness.

When she next woke she was in his arms, held against his chest, his stride long and effortless, and his expression tender and indulgent. She sighed sleepily. What must it be like to be loved and adored by this man?

Why don't you ask the woman he built the ballroom for?

Her good mood instantly evaporated and she stiffened and said, "I'm not an invalid, I can walk."

His honey-gold eyes sparkled. "And here I was enjoying our quiet moment together."

"You should have known better," she retorted. As she wiggled to get out of his grasp, he placed her gently onto her feet. Only then was she aware of the vast corridor with its subtle lighting that showcased huge pillars, the gold walls featuring dark, hand painted hunting scenes

Her breath caught. "So this is the infamous palace of Chawait."

He nodded. "It is." He glanced around, as though seeing it from her eyes. "You get used to its...grandeur." He exhaled then said, "But for now let's freshen up and enjoy some dinner. I'm sure you must be as hungry as you are tired."

Her stomach chose that moment to gargle, and he laughed a little before escorting her through the huge palace. She saw only a handful of servants who looked quietly busy attending to their chores. Water burbled from fountains and huge urns in various rooms. It seemed the liquid gold wasn't a scarcity out here in the desert. Blue and white mosaic tiles revealed the more traditional rooms of the palace, while swirling polished concrete that sparkled with gold highlights showcased the modern areas.

"This way," he murmured smoothly, taking her through an arched doorway and into a mammoth room that was majestic with its many patterned colors. The ceiling of a huge domed roof showcased intricate colors and patterns from where a chandelier the size of a car hung, its glittering, icicle pieces of baccarat crystal, drawing the eyes upward.

He waved a hand at the many seating areas. "We call this the 'meeting room' for obvious reasons."

She looked around. Priceless vases and handcrafted metal sculptures helped to fill in some of the cavernous room, and though the pieces should have looked odd together, somehow they were the perfect, harmonious blend. And yet he didn't trumpet his wealth, there was a subtlety to it, a tantalizing restraint. He must have used an incredible interior designer.

It would take weeks to take in all the intricate details of the room let alone every room of every wing in the palace. Yet although it was a well-known fact Dhamar was seriously wealthy, even by sheikh standards, the grandeur he'd mentioned was as much about the sheer scale of his palace as it was about its opulence.

He nodded to the opposite arched doorway. "Your room is that way."

She followed him, their footsteps echoing eerily in the vast room. Stepping into yet another large corridor, she glimpsed a courtyard through shuttered arched windows on one side, then Dhamar swung open a door on the other.

"Your room, princess."

Her eyes widened. Not even her bedroom suite back home compared to this sumptuousness. From the ankle-deep cream carpet to the colorful mosaic ceiling high overhead, and the huge four-poster bed with its pulled back cream-woolen throw that looked too much like an invitation to snooze...or to fuck.

She sucked in a horrified breath. What was she thinking?

"Are you not pleased with your room?"

She dragged in another breath, one that brought with it a semblance of composure. It didn't make her body or her mind any less attuned to him. "Of course I am," she croaked. "It's...lovely."

He smiled. "I had this updated just recently. You have an adjoining sitting room, a theater, a private indoor pool and spa, and of course a bathroom with all the amenities you need."

"I won't be staying long enough to appreciate it all."

He raised a dark brow. "Surely long enough to take Black Zippy for a few decent rides?"

Despite her effort to be ungracious, excitement coursed through her. How had she forgotten about her gift from Dhamar? "Long enough to ride her," she conceded. "Then I'll be returning home."

A knock sounded on the front door to her suite of rooms. "That will be your luggage," Dhamar said. He walked to the door, opened it, and then nodded for the servants waiting on the other side to bring in her dozen pieces of luggage where they deposited them in a huge walk-in-closet.

She followed the servants past expansive hanging spaces and shoe racks that lined the bottom and middle tiers. There were too many compartments even for all her shoes. Then she stepped into a gorgeous dressing room featuring a pretty white dresser with an intricate shaped mirror and surrounding lights. Much of her paraphernalia could be stored in its drawers. A padded seat beckoned her to sit and put on her makeup or style her hair.

Dhamar moved to stand next to her with a satisfied smile as his efficient team of servants unpacked her bags and placed her clothes carefully onto hangars and into appropriate drawers. Her jewelry pieces went into velvet-lined, glass compartments.

He nodded to a door at the end of her dressing room. "Your bathroom can be accessed through there too, if you wish."

The servants completed their task and quietly left the dressing room, and he took her hand and led her back through the now partly-filled closet and into her bedroom. Then stepping through another arched doorway, they entered a lovely sitting room with windows showcasing a courtyard outside.

He pointed at a door that was all but hidden between some bookcases at the end of a small hallway. "If I'm not here after you've freshened up, I'll be in my adjoining suite of rooms. If you need me, knock on that door. Or come in...either way."

"You're right next door to me?" she asked on a high-pitched squeak.

He nodded. "Of course. Your safety is my priority. Having you close means my men can more easily protect you. There is even an attached panic room if it's needed."

She gaped. "You've thought of everything, haven't you?"

"You can never be too safe, princess."

She had nothing to say to that. Instead she said in a vague voice, "I might go have that shower."

"Then if you'll excuse me, I might go have one myself."

Her stomach pulled at the visual immediately filling her head of him scrubbing his naked, hard body while suds dripped down his contours. And all she could do was nod before he stalked away from her and toward his interconnecting door. Then turning and sending her a little salute goodbye, he disappeared into his suite of rooms.

Chapter Eight

Aisha didn't want to leave the hot shower. But she'd already soaped every inch of her skin until she was almost red, and with the suds now floating down the drain there was no reason to delay the inevitable.

Having dinner with Dhamar was going to be awkward. Much of her self-confidence had disintegrated thanks to Tabari's cavalier treatment. That Dhamar showed interest in her while having another woman on the side made her feel second-best all over again and even more insecure.

She wrapped a big fluffy bath towel around her body and stepped out of the gorgeous mosaic tiles and onto the fluffy white carpet of the closet. Dressing into a pale blue abaya that was embroidered with the same sky-colored flower stitching, she slipped on some silver strappy shoes and then sat on the padded chair to brush out her hair, catching it back into a damp braid before pinning on a matching hijab.

Applying some kohl to her upper and lower lash line, she put on lipstick then leaned back in her chair to look at her reflection, more than happy with what she saw. She was appropriately dressed for a sheikha, demure and yet sophisticated and refined.

Just exactly what Dhamar expected from her.

Except this wasn't her! And now that she wasn't even in her own country she was at liberty to be more...progressive. Wasn't she? She sniffed. She wasn't here to please Dhamar. She was here because he'd blackmailed Tabari to get off the island and away from her.

Taking off her abaya she riffled through her hangers and rejected every modest garment she found. It wasn't until she'd pawed through her carefully folded clothes in her drawers that she found something that perfectly suited her mood.

The long, silky white nightie might reach her ankles but it fitted her body like a glove. The material was almost diaphanous, with a band of intricate lace across her bodice that just barely concealed her breasts and her erect nipples that tightened with anticipation for the night ahead.

Unpinning her hijab, she then undid her braid and shook out her wavy dark hair, the damp ends touching her waist. She smiled, her heart thumping at her sudden change of heart. Her outfit was risqué but it was also liberating, and it made her feel alive all over again.

Pushing some gaudy, yet no doubt outrageously expensive drop silver earrings into her lobes, she stepped out of the walk-in-closet and back through her bedroom. She frowned. Was really expected to knock on his interconnecting door?

She walked into the sitting room and found him idly waiting for her, a drink in hand. His eyes widened at seeing what she was wearing and for the first time she had second thoughts about her controversial outfit. Until he said huskily, "Don't you look good enough to eat."

Warmth flooded through her body and centered between her thighs, a rush of moisture there making her realize just how easily she succumbed to his vocal mastery. It was surely better than any foreplay? That he'd also managed to bring back some of her self-confidence meant everything.

She smiled as she glanced at his more formal attire of black slacks and a dark blue dress shirt. The color set off his golden skin perfectly, highlighting his powerful physique, his sinful handsomeness.

Had she ever seen him in a thobe? He clearly preferred his western attire. She didn't half-mind it, either. But then she doubted a man had ever looked half as sexy as he did right now.

She cleared her throat. "You didn't eat much on the flight here."

"And you ate nothing." He drained his drink and put the crystal glass onto a little table next to his overstuffed chair. "I'd offer you a drink but I'm certain you must be ravenous."

Yes, but not for food.

She ignored the snide little voice inside her head, and instead said with as much grace as she could muster, "I *am* rather hungry."

He held out his arm and she clasped it, so aware of his height and his breadth, of his intriguing scent of ocean and mahogany that she had no doubt had been crafted especially for him. It was his signature scent, as familiar to her now as it was tantalizing and sexy.

She swallowed heavily as she fell into step beside him, aware he was shortening his stride for her slower pace. What was wrong with her? She was falling right into his big, capable hands. He was in love with another woman! Aisha wasn't even on his radar. He'd simply felt compelled to look after her since he'd chased off Tabari.

Ugh. He really was a piece of work. She was all too quickly forgetting his agenda. *And what agenda* is *that exactly?*

Her brother clearly despised Tabari. She wouldn't be surprised if Dhamar had done Hamid a favor by getting rid of Tabari once and for all. It didn't matter how she felt about it. She was just a woman, after all, and women might be valued by their men, but their opinions all too often went unheard.

Hamid might be more progressive than most other sheikhs but he was still over-protective of her. That he'd let her come here unescorted still blew her mind, no matter how much he clearly trusted Dhamar with her.

Ignoring the abstract artwork that undoubtedly cost a fortune on one side of the walls as he led her past the shuttered windows of a courtyard on another, they took yet another corridor before she looked up at him and asked, "Just how big is your palace?"

"It's palatial," he responded with a wry smile. I tend to stick with this side of the palace and its courtyards. Otherwise I'd spend most of my day walking from one end to the other."

She was surprised when he stepped through an archway into an intimate dining room with a six seater table and mosaic walls, the back wall featuring a small waterfall that trickled sweetly into an urn beneath. It was an even bigger surprise to see a spry lady already seated at the head of the table, her traditional abaya and hijab making Aisha suddenly, uncomfortably aware of her own choice of wardrobe.

"Mother," Dhamar said warmly. "I'm so glad you could join us."

"I wouldn't miss this for the world," she said in a dry voice. She stared at Aisha, then smiled a secret smile. "You aren't anything like I was expecting," she said with an arched brow.

"I didn't know I *was* expected by anyone here," Aisha said coolly, despite her suddenly sweaty palms.

"Oh, you were expected, it was just a matter of *when.*"

Aisha looked between the older woman and Dhamar, confused by the cryptic answer and even more confused by the sudden tension between mother and son.

His mother stood. "I'm Sheikha Samaira. It's lovely to finally meet you."

Aisha bowed her head, as was custom. "It is lovely to meet you, too. I've heard a lot about you."

Samaira laughed. "Don't believe all the rumors and conjectures. I'm happier here in Chawait than I ever was in Ishmat, though not because Jamal didn't treat me with the utmost respect. Jamal and Dhamar's father was a piece of—"

"Let's not go there, Mother." He drew Aisha toward the chair right next to his mother's, pulled it out for her, then took the seat opposite.

"Oh, boo. There is nothing wrong with venting if it's the truth, is there?" his mother asked.

Dhamar frowned. "There is when the person in question is dead and unable to defend himself."

Samaira sat back down, her silver bangles tinkling like wind chimes. "I'm only glad neither you nor Jamal take after your father. Now *that* would have broken my heart."

Aisha smiled encouragingly at Samaira. "I never met Dhamar's father."

"You should count yourself as lucky, he—"

"Let's eat, shall we," Dhamar cut in.

Three servants immediately appeared, each carrying a bowl and small, decorative plate. Aisha's mouth watered at the lentil soup with its side of pita bread that was placed in front of her. She devoured it even as Samaira ate sparingly. The next dish was chicken and rice with a side of fattoush salad.

"So tell me about yourself?" Samaira asked Aisha, her dark eyes glinting and her next course barely touched. "And how do you feel about Dhamar?'

Dhamar sighed heavily. "Perhaps just one question at a time. And I'm not sure you're ready to hear how Aisha feels about me just yet."

Samaira laughed huskily. "Perhaps that is why you are so interested, then? There is nothing quite like the chase."

Aisha almost choked on a piece of chicken. She put down her fork as she coughed delicately. "I'm not sure what you've heard, Samaira, but Dhamar has never been interested in me. He has another...love interest."

"Is that so?" Samaira asked, her shrewd dark eyes turning to her son. "Why have I not heard of this lady friend?"

Aisha turned all her attention to Dhamar, too, a masochistic side of her also wanting to know about his latest woman.

Dhamar smirked, a single dimple appearing in his cheek. "There is really nothing to tell." He glanced at Aisha. "I think you were mistaken."

"You've built a ballroom, have you not?"

He nodded. "I have."

Samaira's shoulders shook as she laughed hard. "Oh, this is gold!"

Dhamar's smirk widened. "I shouldn't find it just as funny, but somehow I do."

Aisha glowered at him. If only she knew of the joke he shared with his mom!

He shook his head, and as though reading her thoughts he said gently, "I don't think you're ready just yet to hear the truth, princess."

Ugh. He really was infuriating!

"How considerate of you to decide for me," she said in her sweetest voice. "Perhaps you should also decide when I'm allowed to see Tabari again?"

He dabbed at his mouth with a napkin. "That would be never."

"Luckily you're not my keeper," she volleyed back.

"This just keeps getting better and better!" Samaira crowed.

"You always did have a warped sense of humor," Dhamar informed his mother in a dry voice, though there was no mistaking his love for her.

Aisha picked up her fork once again and concentrated on her food. Anything to gain back control of her composure. What did she care if he'd found a woman he cared deeply about?

He. Meant. Nothing. To. Her.

His mother reached for a fancy, inscribed silver pitcher. "Aisha, would you care for some arrack?"

She picked up her glass and nodded. "Please."

After his mother poured it all the way to top, Aisha swigged down the date liquor like it was water. Dhamar frowned faintly her way. But then he knew she wasn't a big drinker, it'd been enough having to watch her brother partake of more than his fair share of arrack. She rarely drank alcohol at all.

It was petty, but she couldn't resist asking for another full glass. Not because she wanted one. It was simply because Dhamar didn't approve. It was kind of nice to get under his skin.

"Goody," Samaira said with a wide smile as she refilled Aisha's glass and then her own. "A drinking partner."

"That's what you said last time Hamid was here. And look how that turned out."

"Hamid is a darling!" Samaira announced dramatically. "If I'd been a decade or two younger—"

"You *do* know you're talking about Aisha's brother?" he cut in with a dry voice.

"Half-sister," Samaira declared airily. "Besides, he is happily married now and has eyes only for his wife." She waved a languid hand. "I might be widowed but I'm not dead. And I certainly don't have to abide by those same strict rules enforced upon our young, innocent girls."

Aisha couldn't help but giggle. She loved that the older sheikha didn't adhere to traditional customs. But then as a widower she was in an enviable position. Aisha chafed against those very same restrictions.

Samaira sucked down her arrack then turned back to Aisha. "How do *you* cope, dear?"

Aisha looked down at her scanty outfit that was barely a dress. "As you can see, not all that well."

It earned her a raucous laugh from the older woman while Dhamar looked at her with a speculative gaze. Did he truly not comprehend what a struggle it was for a woman of her position? And yet she was fortunate compared to many others. Her biggest gripe was the need to dress and act appropriately to please her people when she simply wanted to throw all that away and be free.

"I understand now what my son sees in you," Samaira said once her laughter finally died off. Her eyes sparkled. "You're the wild filly he'd love to break, a challenge he'd love to solve."

Dhamar put down his fork, his voice patient, subdued. "I think there is quite a bit more to it than that, Mother." He looked at Aisha. "But speaking of fillies...how does a ride early tomorrow morning sound?"

It was the perfect distraction. Horse riding gave her a freedom nothing else did. "On Black Zippy?"

He nodded. "It's why I bought her for you."

"Oh, not tomorrow, Dear. The market is on with all its entertainment." Samaira looked from one to the other. "Surely the ride can wait?"

Aisha swallowed her disappointment, then shrugged and said drily, "What's one more day?" She did love markets and she'd never been to one in Dumak. She'd heard they had the most diverse and interesting stalls as well as entertainment.

Dhamar smiled. "Well then, I can't argue with that. And I'd be pleased to show you around the palace grounds once all the stalls are setup."

She arched a brow. "You have the markets here at the palace?"

He nodded. "Yes, we're only half-an-hour drive from the nearest city, and with tourists flocking here to get an eyeful of the palace exterior, I've never had a lack of people wanting to sell their wares."

Samaira nodded. "Luckily it's only a once-a-month event. I'd simply die otherwise trying to resist spending my son's money."

"That isn't a problem you have to worry about," Dhamar murmured. He looked as Aisha. "Not for my mother or any of my guests."

Aisha sipped some more of her arrack. "Then it seems I've arrived at just the right time."

Samaira snorted and winked. "Then you'd best take advantage of my son's generosity and see that he takes you to the jewelry stall, they have some lovely little gold trinkets there."

Aisha grinned. "I might just do that."

Chapter Nine

Aisha secured her mint green hijab with some pins, then leaned back in her chair to look into the mirror. Her brother, Hamid, would be proud. She looked about as conservative as she'd ever been.

She snorted. At least the mint green color suited her. And the scattering of tiny pearls in both her hijab and matching abaya took the outfit to the next level. Though it pained her to admit it, she did want to make a good impression.

Pushing on some little heeled sandals, she rose from the dresser's chair and padded out through her closet and bedroom, then into the sitting room and toward the door that connected Dhamar's suite of rooms to her own. She lifted a hand, then paused. Was she being too forward?

The door abruptly opened, Dhamar standing in front of her dressed in a white thobe and trousers, along with a keffiyeh headdress. She gulped. She'd wondered what he'd look like in traditional clothes, and now she knew. He was simply gorgeous! And so damn strong and tall, she felt even more dwarfed by him.

His honey brown eyes darkened. "Good timing, again." He stepped through and shut the door behind him before she'd even managed to sneak a peek at his suite of rooms. "Though it's only a short walk to the markets, it's hot enough outside to warrant having a driver take us there."

"Sounds like a good idea. I'm sure we will be doing enough walking once we're at the markets."

He nodded. "We will."

It was only once they stepped outside and walked down a dozen marble stairs that she had a chance to look back and admire the sheer scale of the desert palace. It gleamed bright white under the oppressive morning sunlight, the architecture that included turrets and domes making the palace appear even more impressive.

Ahead of them, the desert could be seen over the top of decorative walls. The sandy wilderness appeared more like a mirage that shimmered in the distance, with a lone eagle flying high in the cloudless blue sky. Water that burbled and cascaded over steps either side of them was stark contrast, reminding her—*any* visitors—that water really was wealth.

They descended the stairs before climbing into a big black SUV that waited for them between two others. She slid into the seat. As Dhamar followed her inside and the driver cruised forward, following the front vehicle, she turned to Dhamar and asked, "More security?"

He grinned. "Be thankful I restrained myself."

"An armored vehicle front and back with bodyguards is restrained?"

"I can't be too careful. The markets are crowded and busy, it's the ideal place for someone to plan an attack."

She leaned back against the buttery seat and closed her eyes. "You know what I hate most about being a sheikha?"

He exhaled softly. "All the constraints?"

She nodded, her eyelashes flickering apart as she looked at him. "I guess if anyone would understand, you would."

He smiled sadly. "Unfortunately, yes. But there are worse things in life."

She snorted. "Sometimes I wish I'd been born a commoner. I itch sometimes to experience true freedom."

He nodded out the window, to where people were filtering inside the tall gates that led into the palace grounds and the market that was set up to one side of the palace. A huge marquee covered many of the stalls, where sellers were already hawking their wares. "Do you really think they have any more freedom than we do?"

She sighed. "I guess not."

"Believe me, they wish more fervently they were us than we'd ever wish to be them." He took her hand and squeezed her fingers reassuringly. "We have a good life, Aisha. Never doubt that."

He had a point. "I guess it's human nature to wish for things we can never have."

His eyes gleamed as he said huskily, "Or to strive to have the things we desperately want."

She blinked at him. Why exactly did he mean by that? And why did she get the bizarre impression he was talking about her? She sniffed. Did he really think she'd fall for his charms when he was planning on marrying another woman? She'd never be second choice ever again.

The driver slowed, then stopped, and as he climbed out to open their back door, Dhamar murmured, "Welcome to the Chawait palace markets."

She smiled, burying her silly thoughts. "Thank you. I look forward to exploring them."

She wasn't lying. The moment she got out of the SUV the anticipation and excitement was tangible. Tourists in bright but modest western clothes were pouring between the stalls along with the locals in their thobes and abayas.

An entertainer at the front juggled swords while balancing on a unicycle. Another juggled blazing torches, before catching each one and swallowing the ends to extinguish the flame. She didn't look away until the juggler with the swords pushed the tip of one down his throat.

At least it made her forget about the security detail following them. It should be easy enough to pretend the guards with their concealed weapons were a part of the crowd, one of many in the sea of faces who attended the markets. She held back an undignified snort. If there was one thing Dhamar and her brother had in common, it was their stringent safety measures.

Walking past the jugglers, she and Dhamar stepped into the front entrance of the market. On one side a nut stall displayed produce in big baskets. Crates of vegetables were stacked high on the other. Farther along bright headscarves competed for space next to big chests of aromatic spices. The scent of cooked meat filled the air from one stall, while halva, a sweet sesame dessert, was sold in another.

"I think some breakfast is in order," Dhamar announced, steering her toward some tables and chairs that took advantage of the marquee's shade.

She sat, content to people watch as Dhamar read out the menu then asked what she'd like. She asked for *mezze,* a breakfast of shared appetizer dishes. She was delighted when a tray was brought out with some of her favorite snacks: bowls of olives, pitta bread, hummus, tabbouleh, pickles, fried eggplant, cheese and nuts.

Choosing a piece of cheese and a stuffed olive from the bowls closest to her, she popped them into her mouth. "Mm."

"That good?"

She nodded. "You have to try them together." She picked up another stuffed olive and selected a piece of cheese and proffered them to him. But what she didn't expect was for him to lean forward and close his mouth over her fingers, sucking the food free.

Her stomach fluttered right along with her heart at the electricity dancing through her nerve endings. It might be inappropriate, but she wanted his mouth on her fingers all over again. Just like she wanted his mouth on hers once more to remind her how great he was at seduction.

She shivered delicately. She'd bet he'd be a master at kissing other, more intimate parts of her body.

What are you doing? He's not yours to fantasize about!

She ignored the voice of reason. Most girls her age were already married and had experienced the wonders of sex. Even her best friend—*ex* best friend—knew now about the act while Aisha had no real idea.

"You're right," he said huskily. She jumped guiltily, as though caught out by her erotic thoughts. Then he added with a glint in his eyes, "That might actually be the best thing I've ever eaten."

Her face heated, her appetite—for food—suddenly non-existent.

He poured some iced water from a jug into her glass. "You look a little hot and bothered."

She gulped the water down. "Must have been the arrack I shared last night with your mother."

"It must have been," he agreed solemnly.

He picked up a piece of triangular pita bread and dipped it into the hummus. "Try this."

She leaned forward and took a bite, then flicked her tongue out to swipe his fingertip.

His eyes heated. "You're playing with fire, princess."

She lifted her chin. "Is it wrong that I want to get burned?"

He sucked in a breath. "Be careful what you wish for, princess, it might come true."

She shivered yet again. And once more it wasn't from fear or rejection. Desire rippled boldly through her body. But although she managed to get her libido under control, it didn't stop awareness from pulsing between them.

Finishing their shared breakfast, they stood in mutual accord and strolled past some more market stalls. The scent of curry wafted toward them, the babble of excited voices and vendors selling their wares filling the air. There was so much to look at her neck was getting sore from craning it every which way.

Then her gaze landed on a stall that showcased gold jewelry on velvet lined trays behind thick glass. She looked up at Dhamar with a wide grin. "Is this the stall your mother mentioned?"

Dhamar didn't appear fazed, in fact he looked rather pleased. "Yes, that would be the one. Let's take a look."

They wandered over and the aged vendor bowed his head, making his pink turban with the feather sticking out of it even more noticeable. He rubbed his bony hands together. "Sheikh Dhamar, welcome to my humble stall. How may I assist you and your lovely friend?"

"Sheikha Aisha and I would like to see your best pieces."

"Of course." He bent, his beaked nose made more prominent as he exhaled with sharp satisfaction before he withdrew a small tray from beneath his counter that was hidden out of sight. "Here we go," he said, and placed it in front of them.

Aisha had a few gorgeous jewelry pieces of her own at home, but even she was impressed by the perfection of the cut diamond drop earrings. The insides sparkled gray and white and the outside reflected a glittering rainbow of colors. "These are beautiful."

Dhamar picked up the white-gold hook of one earring and held it up against her ear. "They would be stunning on you."

She arched a brow. "Are you offering to buy them?"

He smiled. "Pick out whatever you like, princess."

"If I remember correctly you've already bought my birthday present."

He nodded. "Then this is an extra treat for having to stay another day."

She looked into the mirror provided by the vendor, admiring the sparkle of the earrings as she held them next to her ears. They would look gorgeous with her dark hair loose and contrasting with them. She glanced at Dhamar. "One extra day hasn't exactly been a hardship."

"Not exactly?" he repeated drily.

She sniggered, then nodded at the vendor and said, "Thank you, I'll take these."

The vendor smiled toothily and placed them in a special velvet box and then into a drawstring velvet bag. He handed them to her. "Thank you Sheikha Aisha, I'm glad these are going to someone who appreciates them." He cleared his throat, his dark eyes moving from her to Dhamar and back again. "If there is any big news to share any time soon I have more exquisite pieces."

"Big news to share?" she asked faintly.

The vendor nodded eagerly. "If I'm not being too forward I've heard Sheikh Dhamar will be announcing news soon of an impending—"

"The earrings will be all for now," Dhamar cut in smoothly. "You will be one of the first to know if there is any news to tell."

The man bowed formerly. "Of course, Sheikh Dhamar. Please forgive me if I've said too much."

"Not at all," Dhamar said. "It interests me to know what my people are saying. For that you have my gratitude."

"As you have mine in return," the vendor said respectfully.

It wasn't until Aisha walked away with Dhamar that she asked stiffly, "What was that all about?"

"Gossip. It spreads like wildfire."

She knew better. He'd built a ballroom for the woman he wanted to marry. That he'd kissed Aisha and was showing her around the marketplace of his palace grounds meant nothing. He was a man, and she'd learned firsthand that men were cheaters and liars.

He caught her hand up and drew her around to face him. "You've gone quiet. Did I say something to offend you?"

She blew out an aggrieved breath, the truth coming out of her in a rush. "Why are you doing this?"

He frowned. "Doing what?"

"Escorting me around your markets, buying me priceless earrings and keeping me close?"

"Why wouldn't I be?"

She shook her head. "You're giving your people the wrong impression! You're giving *me* the wrong impression."

"And what impression is that, princess?"

Whatever self-confidence she'd built up in the interim with him was slowly leaking out of her. "That you're interested in me...that we're in some kind of a-a relationship."

His eyes darkened, and though the markets were crowded with people, suddenly it was just him and her in a bubble of their own making. "And that bothers you?" he asked softly.

She nodded. "Of c-course it does! I won't be second best ever again, Dhamar. Not like I was with Tabari."

Dhamar's hand tightened on hers. "You'll never be second best with me."

Her voice rose. "Then what of the ballroom you built?" She swallowed back her agitation, and said more quietly, "What about the woman you intend to marry?"

Dhamar drew her closer, their bodies separated by millimeters. "When are you going to realize, princess, the only woman I want to marry is *you*."

Chapter Ten

Aisha swayed, her breath catching at the back of her throat as she struggled to make sense of his words. Surely he wasn't serious? Except she'd never seen him more serious in the four years she'd know him. From his mesmerizing, intent stare, to his tall, forbidding body that seemed perched on a knife's edge as he waited for her reaction.

"You mean that, don't you?" she asked, her voice shaky.

He nodded. "With everything I have. Aisha, I've wanted you from the day I saw you. But you were only sixteen; far too young and impressionable. I had no choice but to wait until you grew into the woman you are now before making you see me beyond being some arrogant sheikh."

"I-I had no idea."

He smiled and nodded. "I was biding my time, waiting for your interest in Tabari to wane."

"And when it didn't you couldn't wait to show me his real nature," she filled in quietly.

"You're right—I couldn't," he admitted. "Though in my defense, I did wait four years before I ran out of patience and decided to reveal his true colors to you. If Tabari had been a decent man I might have found the strength to walk away and give you the happily ever after you deserved. But he was far from decent and you deserved so much better."

"And *you* were the so much better I deserved?"

He nodded, his jaw firm and his tone resolute. "Yes."

Everything finally made so much sense. From the private joke he'd shared with his mom, to Samaira's words that now echoed in her head. *Oh, you were expected, it was just a matter of when.* Even the jewelry vendor had mentioned announcing news of an impending—something. A logical person would fill in that gap as marriage.

The truth left her reeling with raw, unfiltered emotions. Emotions so powerful she could barely process them.

Then he whispered her name and they gravitated closer together before she lifted her head and he lowered his, their mouths meeting in the middle. She moaned against his velvety soft lips, so lost to him in that moment she didn't at first hear the faint gasps and then the cheers from the people around them until it was too late.

She pulled back, aware of the scandal this would cause. But as she refocused on Dhamar he smiled unashamedly and said, "All I ask is that you give me a chance over the next few days."

It seemed natural then for his arm to move around her shoulders as they stepped forward. But she was barely aware of the crowd or the market anymore. All her senses had latched onto the man cradling her close to his side. From his height to his unique mahogany and sea scent and the power he radiated.

That they fitted so perfectly together was just another piece to the illogical puzzle that now made so much sense. Why hadn't she noticed him instead of Tabari?

Dhamar was always on your radar, you just chose to ignore him over a man you thought was more suitable. An older, more devoted and marriageable partner.

How wrong she'd been! Tabari couldn't have been more unsuitable for her if he'd tried. If it wasn't for his affair with Zania she might never have realized her mistake until it was too late.

And you would never have given the right man the chance to prove himself worthy.

She bit her bottom lip, then looked up at Dhamar and asked, "You really built that ballroom for me—for us?"

"I did."

"I can't believe I got everything so wrong."

"I should have told you, but I didn't want to scare you away. Not while you were still so into Tabari and—"

"Hating on you?" she filled in. At his wry nod, she added, "I should have known better. I guess being so protected all my life hasn't helped when it comes to men."

He drew her closer and bent to kiss the top of her head. "I could see you rebelled against the strictures placed on you as a sheikha. I don't doubt for a second that is part of why you chose Tabari."

She shuddered. Was Dhamar right? Had she chosen Tabari in an attempt to rebel against her brother and the edicts of being a sheikha? "I was blind to what was right in front of me."

"No. You were young and still learning from your mistakes, in just the same way Zania learned from hers."

Aisha sighed heavily. "I owe Zania an apology, don't I? If it wasn't for her mistake my life might now be a whole lot different."

And not in a good way.

"I believe you were both victims. The only villain is Tabari. He took advantage of you both."

"Yet I blamed Zania for everything." She shook her head. "I hope she can forgive me."

"The blame isn't yours to bear," Dhamar reminded. "Tabari knew exactly what he was doing."

She leaned her head on his shoulder, loving their connection, their closeness. "I should have listened to you sooner."

"You're hearing me now...I can't ask for more than that." He guided her toward a nearby dessert van. "If there is one thing I've learned from my mistakes—and there have been a lot of them—it's that ice-cream fixes everything."

Despite everything she giggled, and was soon choosing a mulberry flavor ice-cream in a cone while he chose vanilla topped with pistachios. After he paid they ate their treats while they stood and watched a snake charmer inside an enclosure. He sat on the ground playing an instrument while a cobra rose from out of a basket, its hood extended as though it was about to strike.

She shuddered a little and Dhamar drew her closer. It was comforting how safe and protected he made her feel, like nothing could touch her while she was with him.

Once they finished their ice-creams, he leaned down, his voice husky and his breath warm next to her ear. "It's been a big day. And I don't just mean the markets. You've had a lot to take in."

She nodded. The truth had hit her hard. She'd considered Dhamar her nemesis all these years when in actual fact he'd been biding his time waiting for her to grow up and enjoy her childhood before seriously pursuing her.

"Let's return to the palace where you can get some much needed rest."

"I'd like that," she admitted.

They drifted away from the snake charmer and the people who'd crowded around to watch, Dhamar choosing a different route as they headed back toward the car so that she could see some more stalls. But she was no longer interested in anything outside of their sphere, she was barely even aware of the security detail that fell in behind them.

Until two large pigs in a small pen ahead suddenly began to fight. One of them panicked and jumped, snapping some of the barricade that restrained it. Aisha froze as it broke free and ran full pelt toward them, its beady eyes wildly glinting.

The world shifted as Dhamar picked her up and swung her out of harm's way, the pig missing his legs by bare millimeters as it continued past.

She drew in a steadying breath, all her senses focusing on the man holding her...the same man who wanted her to be his wife. She was only half-aware some of his security team had restrained the pig, which was now squealing and carrying on about its capture.

She was too busy enjoying her own capture.

Though her emotions swirled all over the place, excitement and anticipation were by far the most powerful. She really had been attracted to Dhamar from the very start, but she'd fought against those feelings. She'd been too terrified to admit her secret fascination—even to herself—and give into temptation.

Dhamar looked down at her as he cradled her against his chest, his gaze suddenly stripped of all defenses yet made unreadable thanks to the emotions brimming in them. "Let's get you out of here," he murmured throatily, his long-legged stride eating up the ground. Minutes later he stepped through the exit and toward their SUV with its patient driver waiting by the rear passenger door.

After Dhamar set her carefully back onto her feet next to the SUV, she sent him a smile. "Thank you...but I'm not made out of glass."

"Then humor me just this once. I lost a good ten years of my life watching that wild pig run toward you. It might have seriously hurt you—or worse."

Her throat dried. He was right. The pig hadn't been domesticated, it had been a feral animal escaping for its life—and she'd been in its way. "You saved me from injury. Who needs a security detail when I have you as my knight in shining armor?"

His stare held hers, and though he looked ready to say more, she wasn't sure if she could take anymore of his honesty. Instead she climbed into the backseat of the SUV and Dhamar immediately followed before the driver shut their door, enclosing them in from the rest of the world.

She hadn't even clicked on her seatbelt when Dhamar gathered her close, cupped her face, then kissed her in the privacy of the vehicle with its tinted windows.

His eyes glowed when he finally pulled back and said huskily, "I'm addicted to kissing you now, princess."

"It's fair to say the feeling's mutual."

He gathered her hand in his then lifted it to kiss her knuckles. "Tell me I haven't scared you away for good."

Something inside her chest softened. "I doubt you'll ever get rid of me now."

The short drive back to the main entrance of the palace was done in silence. While Aisha was wholly conscious of the man beside her, she'd never been more self-aware in her life. There was a sense of breathless anticipation, of a brewing, unstoppable storm.

After getting out of the SUV and climbing the stairs hand-in-hand, she was in such a daze she could only be thankful for Dhamar's guidance as he led her through the palace corridors and finally into her own suite of rooms.

He turned to her and brushed a hand down her cheek. "Will you be okay?"

Did he mean apart from the fact her emotions were about as volatile and unpredictable as they'd ever been? "I'll be fine," she lied.

His gaze narrowed a little, his honey-gold stare darkening. "You know where to find me if you need me."

She blinked. Did he mean that literally or was she reading too much into his words? "You're going now?"

He exhaled slowly. "If I don't leave now I might never go." He stepped back, as though touching her and being so close would prove it. "I'll see you tonight at dinner."

He pivoted and stepped toward the sitting room and his interconnecting door. He was halfway there when she called out, "Dhamar...wait." When he paused, then turned her way, she added, "Don't go. I-I need you."

Chapter Eleven

Dhamar stood poised on the precipice between duty and desire. But there really was no contest. He'd withheld from temptation for too long already. "Are you sure?" he croaked. "Once I touch you there might be no going back."

She unpinned her hijab and tossed it aside, her dark eyes glinting with passion. "I'm sure."

It was like a race gun going off in his head. One second he was standing fully dressed, the next he'd thrown off his thobe, keffiyeh and pants, and he was scooping Aisha up in his arms before striding with her toward her bed.

He laid her down on the luxurious mattress, her parted lips like magnets to his mouth. He groaned as he kissed her long and deep, his hands moving all over her body, touching her...undressing her.

Her lashes fluttered when he bared her to his gaze, and he loved that there was no shame in her response. She'd completely yielded to him, her arms now above her head and her back arched, pushing her quivering breasts with her tempting pink nipples even closer to him.

He didn't need to be asked twice. Abandoning her delectable mouth, he bent his head and sucked the nipple of one breast into his mouth, swirling his tongue around the areola. She arched higher and he gently nipped. She stiffened and gasped, relaxing only once he'd kissed away the sting then started on her other breast.

That she was so responsive told him exactly what he already knew. She was a passionate woman buried beneath the reserves of not just being a female, but a sheikha, too. But though in public she might have to present a modest façade, in the bedroom she could be someone else entirely. And he'd do everything in his power to bring out her real and passionate side.

Her true identity.

His own control slipped when she reached for him and glided her hands down his sides and to his buttocks, electricity sizzling through his entire body. It wasn't until she reached out a tentative hand and touched his dick that his breath hissed out and he stiffened, his libido skyrocketing out of control.

"Am I doing something wrong?" she asked, her innocence hitting him once again. She really had no idea what she was doing to him.

He shook his head. "Believe me, you're do everything right."

She slid her hand up and down him. "You're so hard and yet so velvety-soft." She bit her bottom lip and added starkly, "But surely you're too big to fit inside me?"

He closed his eyes, his jaw locking tight and his willpower stretched to the limits. How could such an innocent touch and question affect him so profoundly? Maybe it was because this wasn't just a physical moment; it was an emotional one, too.

His feelings for Aisha hadn't diminished over time, they'd strengthened. This moment was a culmination of everything he felt for her. And he planned to show her exactly how much he adored her.

"I'll make you so wet all you'll feel is a momentary discomfit." She blinked suspiciously, and he added softly, "Trust me."

She nodded, and said softly, "I do trust you."

A part of him melted even before he moved down her body and kissed her cute little navel with its gem piercing. Her body quivered and he couldn't help but smile at the torment he was about to inflict on her.

He moved lower until he was between her thighs. Parting her outer folds like petals to a flower, he exposed her gorgeous clit that was already plumped with passion. He exhaled, his breath sweeping across the sensitized bud.

"Oh..."

Her wonderment was just the beginning. He leaned close to lick her flesh and she jerked and groaned. He didn't give her a chance to grow used to it. He went in for the kill, licking and sucking and drawing on her bud for long minutes until she shattered under his mouth and cried out his name.

He inhaled her eau-de-orgasm bouquet. The musky scent was incredible and set off every one of his erogenous buttons. He needed her now...yesterday.

Climbing back up her body while little after-tremors shook her body, he guided his shaft between her thighs, and plunged in deep. Her shock was absolute: from soft and welcoming to stiff and unyielding.

He leaned down and kissed her, waiting until she softened beneath him before he drew back and said, "The worst is over, princess. The best is yet to come."

"I-I want to believe you," she muttered. "But my body says otherwise."

"Then let's change your body's mind."

He kissed her once more before he withdrew part-way, and gently rocked back inside. He repeated the action over and over until her stare went from wide-eyed shock to slumberous within minutes. She might have been a virgin, but her passionate nature meant she was never going to rebel against sex.

He rocked a little faster, her strangled gasp soon turning into little moans of need. "I never expected to like it this much," she admitted in a small, mystified voice.

He closed his eyes against her naked, sex-tousled look. It was hard enough not to ejaculate just from the feel of possessing her. Seeing her stunned awe had his balls lifting and his seed ready to explode.

Then she wrapped her legs around his hips and embraced their lovemaking, her voice challenging when she said, "I want you to give me everything you've got."

His heart beat drummed in his ears as adrenaline surged. "Be careful what you wish for, princess."

She didn't have time to argue the point. He stroked long and deep inside her, and as she mewled without restraint his own restraints fell away and he drove into her harder and faster...until sensation swept them both up and she orgasmed hard around his shaft, forcing his own release to detonate inside her.

It was in that moment that he knew without a doubt...Aisha was his one and only.

His everything.

Chapter Twelve

Aisha had no idea she'd fallen asleep until she woke up with Dhamar bent over her, kissing her awake. That his lips on hers felt so right—dominating and yet soft and supple—made her question everything she'd imagined about Tabari.

Had she ever really loved him? Because suddenly the feelings she thought she'd had seemed silly and inconsequential compared to the depth of feelings she had for Dhamar. Though it seemed impossible, in just a few days he'd become her moon and her stars...her world.

That she was close to handing her heart to him and trust in him completely made her either the biggest risk taker or a gigantic fool. She guessed only time would tell which one. But for now she wanted to float on the cloud of satisfaction they'd created together.

He straightened, and it took her a moment to realize he was dressed in smart gray slacks and a red dress shirt. "How are you feeling, sleepyhead?" he asked.

She stretched, then grimaced a little at her overstretched and sore muscles. It didn't take away from the blissful cloud she continued to float on, the happiness emanating from her. That she'd thought his sexy voice had to be better than any foreplay was laughable now. His skill in the bedroom was nothing short of miraculous. "I don't know that I've ever felt better," she admitted.

He grinned like a Cheshire cat, his satisfaction all too clear. "We're good together, princess."

She smiled right back. "We are, aren't we?"

He curled a piece of her long dark hair around his thumb and forefinger, touching it reverently before tucking it behind her ear. "If you're not too tired we're due to have dinner in half-an-hour." He cocked a brow. "Though I'm sure my mother wants to drill us both on our day at the markets as much as she wants to eat."

Aisha sat, then realized she was still nude—of course she was!—when the top sheet fell away and her breasts were in full view. Her nipples pebbled at his dark stare and she had to resist covering up until the moment he groaned and said, "You're perfect."

Her face heated, any insecurity melting clean away. "You know all the right words to say."

He caught her hand in his and pressed it to his swollen groin. "My body doesn't lie."

She swallowed hard. Despite her body's twinges she was instantly wet, and his nostrils flared at her aroused scent, his grip on her hand tightening.

Then he stepped back and said, "As much as I want you right now, your body needs time to get used to mine."

"So why is it telling me it's ready for you right now?" she asked sweetly.

His breath hissed and his eyes glinted. "As much as I love your passionate nature, it's overriding cold hard logic. I won't hurt you, Aisha."

She admired his restraint, she really did. But it didn't mean she had to take it lying down. She flipped aside the cover and stood proudly naked in front of him. "Then I guess I'd better go take a shower."

She sashayed away from him and into the adjoining bathroom, aware of his eyes following her the whole way until she was out of sight. She smiled widely. His admiration made her feel sexy and confident after much of her self-empowerment had been stripped away thanks to Tabari's disregard.

It was only when she turned on the shower and glanced down to find not even a drop of virginal blood on her thighs that she realized Dhamar must have cleaned her while she'd slept. It made her heart pitter-patter a little harder for him. He was a sheikh; he had servants and staff to do his every bidding. And yet he'd given her all his attention.

She stepped into the shower, the water that tumbled over her still-heated and sensitive skin arousing her all over again and making her deaf to Dhamar's tread behind her. She closed her eyes, her heavy sigh morphing into a groan the moment Dhamar's big hands curled around her shoulders, his even bigger cock pressing into the small of her back.

"You're like a siren calling to me," he growled. "I can't keep away."

He pulled her tighter against him, her spine to his front. She tilted her head back, his mouth then covering hers, dominating their kiss while he parted the petals of her folds and bared her clit to his touch. She moaned into his mouth, their tongues tangling and their lips mashing while he deftly massaged.

This was no gentle foreplay. She was as desperate for him as he clearly was for her, the rivulets of water running down their bodies only enhancing their urgency.

Then he tore his mouth away from hers and spread his legs wide apart. "Bend over," he commanded.

Excitement pulsed through her, his demand alone making her wet. When he entered her from behind, though she was stretched to the limits, there was no more pain, only mind-blowing sensation. His thrusts made her breasts bounce while his balls slapped rhythmically, her inner tightness creating a friction that generated instant heat.

Heaven help her, it was all too much. Too intense. Too hot. Too...everything. She lasted a minute, maybe two, before a powerful orgasm rippled through her in a shockwave of heat that pushed her off the edge of the cliff and left her soaring.

She vaguely heard someone shouting out Dhamar's name, then realized it'd come from her own lips. She'd been so lost in the moment she'd become someone else. No, she'd finally become herself, exposed both figuratively and literally.

The epiphany hit her even as Dhamar thrust once, twice, then grunted long and loud, his seed pulsing inside her and his hands crushing her against him.

Afterward there were gentle touches and lingering kisses while the shower washed away all evidence of their tryst. But he seemed just as disinclined to leave their blissful bubble as she was.

He cupped her face, his eyes holding hers. "You're mine now," he said huskily, the water pouring over them an orchestra to his vow. "No one will ever tear us apart."

Once upon a time his words might have infuriated her. Now they were gloriously reassuring. She needed to know she was important. She wanted to hear she was special to him, worthy of being his lover.

She stood on tiptoe and kissed him, showing him without words she wanted that too. It took all the willpower she possessed to break the kiss and drop back onto the flat of her feet. "I believe we have a dinner date?"

"I believe you're right." He flipped off the torrent of water and slid a hand through his black, wet hair before he chuckled darkly. "This is going to be an interesting meal."

Forty minutes later she sat in front of her dresser mirror. She'd braided her damp hair and hidden it beneath a pretty lilac hijab, her achingly sore yet buzzing body swathed in a matching abaya featuring lilac and white embroidered flowers. Slipping her feet into heeled shoes, she walked toward the man who made her heart beat faster just being near him.

It'd taken Dhamar no time to dress back into the same slacks and dress shirt he'd stripped off before joining her in the shower. Except now he looked impossibly even more handsome with his damp hair and a cat-that-ate-the-canary smile, his teeth flashing white beneath his designer stubble.

He cocked his head to the side. "I don't know that I've ever seen you look more beautiful."

She giggled. "Are you taking all the credit?"

"For your sexual glow? Hell, yes."

"Well I guess that honor *is* yours," she conceded. She pressed a hand to her brow. "Do you think your mom will notice?"

He grimaced. "I'd hate to break it to you, but there is very little my mother misses."

He reached for her hand, and she took comfort from his strength and his warmth. As long as she had him by her side she could face anything, even his eagle-eyed mother.

Samaira was sipping on some arrack when they arrived. She gaped when she saw them, then broke into a huge grin, her eyes sparkling. "I knew it!"

"Knew what, Mother?" he asked wryly.

"I knew the rumors circulating about you two at the markets *weren't* rumors!"

Dhamar drew out a chair for Aisha and took the one opposite her and next to his mother. "Since when do you listen to gossip?"

"Since my son confessed to me four years ago about the woman he wanted to marry and I've been waiting...and waiting ever since for that to happen."

Aisha's face heated even as a tingling of emotion poured through her. He'd really waited four years for her. It seemed almost too surreal to believe.

Samaira glanced at Aisha. "You're looking all...loved up."

Dhamar groaned. "Must you?"

"What?" Samaira grinned. "You two have clearly been...occupied. It doesn't take a genius to figure out why you two are so late for dinner." Her bangles chimed as she lifted her hand and took a deeper drink of her arrack. "Of course, this means we will have to bring the wedding forward. We can't have a pregnancy before marriage."

Aisha gasped. She hadn't even considered the fact they hadn't used protection. She'd been so naïve and swept up in the moment, her inexperience no doubt laughable to someone of Dhamar's capabilities.

"Don't sound so shocked!" Samaira admonished. "Even someone of your innocence must know how babies are made." She looked smug. "And I have no doubt you and my son will give me the most gorgeous grandchildren."

The servants came out then with their first course. But Aisha was suddenly no longer hungry. She pressed a hand to her stomach. Was it possible she'd already conceived? All she'd ever wanted was a family, she'd just never suspected it would be with someone other than Tabari.

Samaira blinked at her. "You really should eat the hummus and mushroom soup. You need to eat nutritious food now and stay healthy."

"Mother, that's enough," he admonished. "Let her live her own life."

Samaira sniffed and pulled away the bottle of arrack. "Well then...at least keep off the arrack and other alcoholic substances until we know for sure."

"That will be easy enough to achieve," Aisha reassured the older woman. She dug a spoon into the bowl of soup and tasted it. It was delicious! It would be no hardship eating it all. "I'm not usually much of a drinker anyway."

That had always been her brother's department. Luckily he abstained now too.

Samaira nodded. "That's good." She sighed. "I guess I should cut back too if I'm to be a long term grandmother."

"Aren't you getting a little ahead of yourself, Mother?" he asked. "It could take years to conceive."

"Nevertheless you took her virginity, did you not?" Samaira asked imperiously. "So the wedding needs to take place sooner rather than later."

Aisha was caught somewhere between excited and overwhelmed. "My brother might have something to say about that," she said weakly.

Dhamar smiled her way. "Your brother has given his full approval."

"Well of course he has!" Samaira announced airily. "Who wouldn't want my son as their future brother-in-law?"

Aisha pushed back her seat and stood, her legs as shaky as her voice. "I don't believe I've been asked to be anyone's bride."

Dhamar's dark eyes glinted. "You're right. I haven't yet officially asked for your hand in marriage." He stood then, his hand going into the pocket of his gray slacks. "Allow me to rectify that."

Aisha put a hand to her chest. Surely he hadn't bought a ring for her already? Surely he wasn't going to propose...now?

He knelt in front of her next to the table, a little velvet box in hand. He opened it to reveal a stunning diamond the size of a small planet. "Aisha, will you do me the honor of becoming my wife?"

She stepped back, her emotions tumbling one after the other. Was this what she wanted? Was *he* what she wanted? After so many years of dreaming about Tabari it was as if all her doubts hit her at once. What is these last few days had been an illusion, the fantasy she'd craved, and she'd yet to think things through with any clarity?

Samaira looked from one to the other. Her stare then slammed into Aisha. "You have doubts?" she asked, voice a little screechy and disbelieving.

Aisha crossed her arms, becoming defensive without even meaning too. "I-I need some time to think about...everything."

Dhamar straightened. "I'm scaring you."

She shook her head. "N-no. I mean yes. I don't know."

He snapped the lid shut. "Don't answer me now, princess. Give it a few days. A few weeks. Hell, six months if that is what it takes. I don't want you to have any doubts. If you want to be my wife it will be forever."

She nodded, relieved and unsettled all at once. Of course she wanted him! But were her feelings for him real? Everything these last few days had happened at warp speed, her feelings jumping from one man to another with too much ease. She wasn't certain she knew anything anymore, including her own feelings.

He smiled gently down at her. "Let's forget dinner tonight and get some sleep, then get out of the palace first thing in the morning. You can take Black Zippy for that ride I promised and I'll bring my stallion, Smoke. I'm betting he needs some exercise too."

She managed to smile back, her doubts dissolving. He really did know her too well. Knew that riding made all her doubts fall away while she experienced freedom like nowhere else. "I'd like that."

Ten minutes later she decided what she didn't like was for him to leave her in her suite of rooms with an almost chaste kiss on her lips before he strode away from her and entered his own interconnecting rooms.

Make up your mind! You either want him or you don't want him. You can't have it both ways!

She snorted, then pivoted away from the doorway leading to his bedroom. A night apart was exactly what she needed...wasn't it?

Chapter Thirteen

For the first time in too long Aisha beamed with joy. There was something glorious about an early morning ride in the great outdoors, with the horses' hooves clopping across the sand and their tails swishing back and forth, while the cool air evaporating fast beneath the heat of a new day.

She glanced at Dhamar. He wore traditional clothes which helped protect him from the heat. His white thobe and his keffiyeh headgear reflected the sun and his long white pants beneath protected his legs from chafing.

That he was a natural horseman shouldn't impress her, but the way he used such gentle hands and legs to keep his huge gray stallion under control was a credit to him. She looked ahead, to where sand dunes gave way to rocky, treed mountains. Though the climb ahead would test the horses' strength and endurance, it would also give them some much needed shade.

She tilted her chin. After last night's involuntary revolt against Dhamar's proposal, she'd been a good little girl staying by his side. But enough was enough. She glanced up at him, her voice thrumming with energy. "Race you to the base of the mountain!"

Before he had a chance to protest she leaned forward, pressed her thighs to her filly's sides and gave her a looser rein. Black Zippy didn't disappoint. She took off until the sandy ground was a blur beneath, her black mane flying with every long stride.

Aisha shouted with glee, adrenaline bursting through her at the sheer speed of her mare beneath. She crooked her neck to look behind. Her eyes widened at the long stride of Dhamar's stallion, which allowed them to cover more ground and slowly gain on them.

Dhamar's eyes glinted dangerously and Aisha hooted with joy and laughter before she faced forward again and urged her mare even faster.

Now *this* was living! No rules, no constraints, just the speed of her horse and the stream of air slipping past.

The mountain loomed before them like a huge sentinel and Aisha crouched low on her mare's wither, giving the mare every advantage to get to the base first. Winning against Dhamar would be quite the achievement!

Then the louder staccato beat of Dhamar's stallion sounded beside her, the big horse keeping pace beside her. Dhamar leaned close and drew on Black Zippy's reins, his other hand reining in his own mount, stopping them both.

She scowled at him as they stopped, the horses blowing and snorting. "You shouldn't have been able to catch me! Black Zippy has—"

"Years before her true potential comes to light," he interjected. He patted his gray stallion on the neck. "Smoke has two years on her and still had trouble gaining on her."

She touched her light-colored hijab, grateful for the soft material that kept the sand out of her hair and her head cool. "You should have kept going. You might have won."

He cocked a dark brow. *"Might* have?" At her snort of disgust, he added, "Tell me you won't ever gallop off alone like that again. If it wasn't for Smoke you might have gotten too far ahead to catch up. As it is we've left our bodyguards far behind."

"Surely it's not the end of the world." She swept a hand out to encompass the desert behind them. "We're in the middle of nowhere out here!"

He narrowed his eyes and nodded at the mountain. "Once we ride up there anyone could be lurking behind the trees and rocks."

She wasn't convinced. Nomads were far less common now with most families choosing to live in the cities where work beckoned. *What about the nomads who attacked your brother in the desert and took Holly?*

She shivered. There were, of course, exceptions to the rule.

Black Zippy tossed her head, her bit jangling. The filly had sensed her rider's sudden nerves, and now Black Zippy had a taste of racing she clearly wanted more. Aisha patted the filly's sweat-lathered neck. "Easy girl, once we go uphill you won't be so eager to run."

Dhamar waited until his five men galloped up and pulled their mounts to a stop before he nodded at them and said, "Let's stay close now and alert."

The swarthy man at front on a fine-boned chestnut with a dish-shaped face and a long, arched neck that was typical of an Arab horse, nodded assent. "Good idea Sheikh Dhamar. There have been sightings recently of unknown men in this area. We can't be too cautious."

Dhamar frowned. "Do you think it's too big of a risk, Manzur?"

Aisha huffed out an annoyed breath. She might be a woman but she wasn't weak. "We're protected, aren't we?" She glanced meaningfully at the swords strapped to the men's backs and the guns holstered at their sides. She'd bet even Dhamar had some kind of weapon under his loose thobe. "What's the worst that could happen?"

"Other than us all dying?" he asked drily.

"You don't really imagine anyone would dare go up against you?"

He shrugged. "Despite my people being aware of my stringent rules against kidnapping, many would still risk it."

She blinked, peering up at the rugged, treed mountain that seemingly beckoned them to climb it. To be so close without enjoying the steep but shady ride and then the beautiful views at top seemed like sacrilege. "Then you're probably right," she said with heavy reluctance. "We should turn back."

"I'll have an army of men scour the mountain tomorrow to make sure it's safe, then we'll go up to the very top, I promise."

She managed a smile. Did she even want to stay an extra day for another ride with potentially spectacular views? *Of course you do.* She'd never had this kind of freedom. It was heady, exciting. Having Dhamar as her guardian wasn't all that bad either.

Having sex with him had changed everything. There was no longer just a spark between them, there was an inferno. She sucked in a breath. When was the last time she'd even thought about Tabari in a romantic sense?

Tabari who? A little voice asked.

She'd hardly even thought about her best friend, Zania. Aisha grimaced. She really had been too hard on her. Zania had been a loyal friend, and until recently, she'd been an innocent young woman who'd been taken advantage of in the worst way possible. Her name would be mud now.

She blew out a breath. Dhamar had been right about Tabari using his charm on Zania, using her...period.

Dhamar lifted his hand in the direction of the palace. "Let's head back."

Whomp.

One of the horsemen cried out at the arrow now sticking through his shoulder. His horse lunged with fright, almost toppling him off, while ten or more arrows flew through the air, one whistling straight past Aisha's face.

Dhamar's whole countenance whitened at Aisha's close call. When dozens of men came running out from their hiding places, brandishing swords and their bows and arrows, he planted his horse in front of hers and shouted, *"Go!"*

Aisha's heart surged into double speed and she leaned low on Black Zippy's neck and pushed her legs hard against the filly's sides to let her know she meant business. The filly folded her ears back and took off, her hooves kicking up sand and her speed soon leaving everyone behind.

Holy shit! Dhamar had been right to be worried. They'd all been in danger. That she might have been kidnapped or worse if he hadn't stopped her at the foothill of the mountain left her shaking, adrenaline pouring through her.

A sob tore free from her throat. She'd wanted action and adventure, but not this kind! Dhamar had risked his life by blocking her from any further arrows.

She looked behind her, seeing the men on their horses. She narrowed her eyes. Where *was* Dhamar? She couldn't even see his big white stallion, Smoke. She slowed Black Zippy even as the other horses thundered past.

Her heart now in her throat, she drew the filly to a stop before turning her back around. Aisha squinted. The stallion lay on the ground near the base of the mountain, Dhamar nowhere in sight. She looked back at his men, all of whom had wheeled their mounts around to come back for her.

She shook her head. "I'm not going anywhere."

The swarthy man, who appeared to be the leader, refused to listen to her. "I'm sorry, Sheikha Aisha, but if I have to force you to come with us, I will. It's too late now for Dhamar."

Her throat closed up as denial swept through her. "What do you mean, too late?" she croaked.

"I mean he's either dead or captured. We were vastly outnumbered and he knew it. He sacrificed himself to protect us. Our only hope now is that they'll keep him alive for a ransom."

Some of the men looked away, one of them muttering, "Even if that's what they want, we can't pay it. Dhamar made it illegal."

"What? What do you mean, illegal?" she asked, her shaky voice outraged. He'd mentioned rules against kidnapping, but not against a ransom. What was the point of having so much money if he couldn't use it to save himself?

The leader sighed uncomfortably. "He put that law in place so that kidnapping wouldn't become so prevalent."

Her throat closed up. He'd no doubt done that after her brother's wife, Holly, had been kidnapped, not to mention Sheikh Mahindar's gorgeous wife, Arabelle. Both women had been lucky to make it out alive.

Would fate have other ideas for Dhamar?

Her whole body clenched with denial, her mind shutting down and refusing to even consider it. Dhamar was strong, powerful, he'd find a way to survive. That he was a sheikh meant he was important enough to keep alive.

Or important enough to kill and make a statement.

No. She wouldn't—couldn't—believe that. There was no way she'd make such a strong connection with a man to then have it taken away from her just as fast. That it'd taken his kidnapping to open her eyes and make her see the truth was nothing short of a slap to her face.

Was it too little, too late?

A whinny sounded and she jerked her gaze to the gray stallion that was now standing on shaky legs. The horse seemed to quickly gain strength and Aisha's heart thundered even as she breathed out, "Smoke is alive!"

The swarthy leader put the tips of his thumb and forefinger into his mouth and whistled. Smoke immediately cantered toward them, holding his majestic white head to one side as his reins dragged along the ground, a trail of blood leaking behind him.

Aisha had no idea why, but seeing Smoke alive gave her hope. She wasn't going to give up on Dhamar. She'd never give up on him again.

Chapter Fourteen

Dhamar tried to stretch his legs, and failed. Not only had the bastards trussed him up like a turkey at Christmas, his cracked ribs prevented any range of motion. They'd done a number on his face, too. He had no doubt his nose was broken, with one eye puffed up so badly he couldn't see out of it. The burning sensation in his wrists from the ropes tied around them was the least of his concerns.

There would be no short term relief. He was even beginning to doubt he'd find relief long term. It'd been—what?—five days? No six, since he'd been shot at with two arrows, one in his thigh and one through his arm.

That his captors had even bothered to pull the arrows out had been as much from the enjoyment of watching him hold back screams as anything else, otherwise why would they have ignored the infection that had set in? He was only lucky the arrowheads hadn't caught on any major arteries on the way back out.

What did it matter? He would be delirious soon, and dead not long after that.

Any hope he'd had of making Aisha fall in love with him and making her his wife was void now. The realization made him suck in a harsh breath, and then let it hiss out slowly thanks to the horrific pain of his cracked ribs.

He'd had such grand plans. As a sheikh very few things he wished for were out of his grasp, but it was now crystal clear he couldn't have everything he wanted in life. He'd soon not even have a life. The possibility was looking more like a probability with each hour, each second that passed.

The leader of the brigand left his group of men he'd been conferring with, strolling over from the campfire they'd set up inside a cave, where minimal smoke, if any, would be seen outside. Dhamar didn't look his way, didn't acknowledge him at all. The man, Issam, was without mercy, and Dhamar had experienced enough of his sadistic punishment.

Issam chuckled softly as he crouched at Dhamar's feet. "It looks like you're more good to us alive than dead, after all."

Dhamar didn't believe a word of it. He'd experienced enough lies from his captives to know they fed him false hope. It seemed mental torture was far more entertaining than physical, and they'd devised enough of both.

Another tread approached, but Dhamar was no longer interested in what was planned for him. Better to die a quick death than suffer endlessly at their hands.

Either way, Aisha was lost to him. If she was smart she would have gotten on the first flight home and scrubbed all her memories of him. He might have become her first lover, but they'd spent too little time together for her to genuinely care about him. That he'd proposed to her and had seriously imagined she'd say yes had been nothing short of madness.

His love for her had blinded him. He'd pushed her too hard.

If he was being honest she probably hated him more than ever now. Despite their intimacy, her heart lay with another man. Dhamar only wished she could see she deserved someone so much better that Tabari.

"We might have left it too late," the stranger mused aloud.

Dhamar looked away from the men until the moment one of them pressed a careful hand around the wound at his thigh. He couldn't stop a moan as the infection around his leg throbbed in sharp agony.

But rather than the kick or punch he'd been expecting for daring to make a sound, the other man released his leg and said softly, "You have nothing to fear from me. I'm a doctor brought here to help you. If you have any fight left in you at all, now is the time to bring it out. I'll do all I can to keep you alive."

Issam exhaled noisily, then spat on the ground near Dhamar's feet. "I'd rather that you suffered some more. But if you die we lose all hope of a ransom." His lip curled in disgust. "Which means I have no choice but to see if you have enough fight in you to live another day." He signaled to one of his other men, who came over with a knife, then sawed at the ropes that bound Dhamar.

He refused to allow hope to cloud his logic. He didn't trust these men one bit. They were as likely to pretend he had a future, then use the same knife to plunge it deep into his chest while watching the light dim from his eyes. He had, after all, signed a clause that said no ransom was to be paid for his return...ever. It would otherwise set a precedent for others to want money for his capture.

But nothing more happened other than the ropes falling away, and his renewed circulation causing sharp pins and needles to go through him in an agonizing rush.

"Get a cloth, soap and hot water," the doctor instructed someone. "We'll need to clean up these wounds."

Dhamar must have wavered in and out of consciousness because he only vaguely recalled the wash down, then the faint prick of a needle as he guessed either pain relief or antibiotics were injected into his bloodstream.

When he woke next the doctor looked haggard but relieved, and offered him a few sips of water. This time when Dhamar groaned it was from the taste of the blessedly cool liquid trickling down his parched throat, not from pain.

He blinked, fighting against a deep longing to give into sleep yet again. He looked blearily around the cave. The fire was out with only a few embers glowing beneath a pile of ash. But going by the bright fingers of sunlight forcing their way inside the gloomy cave, he guessed it had to be mid-morning.

His captors were nowhere to be seen.

His heartbeat surged. Now was his chance to ask some questions. "Why am I being released? I mean, why now? It's against the law to pay for my ransom."

The doctor smiled, his brown eyes glinting. Not with kindness exactly, but a spark of sympathy. "Your country may have their hands tied, but the Sheikha of Imbranak was under no such constraints."

Dhamar's whole body clenched, and he cursed as pain swept through him. He was a long way off being fully healed. Guess his captors must have known it too or they would never have left him alone with only the doctor for company. Not that he cared about any of that just yet.

A fragile bubble of optimism was growing inside him, feeding him hope. He quashed the emotion as he admitted gruffly, "Aisha barely sees me as more than a friend." *Nemesis* was her word of choice. That she'd refused to marry him hurt more than he cared to admit, even to himself. "I doubt she'd empty her bank account for me."

The doctor set up another injection. "For the pain," he advised. As he pushed it into him, the doctor explained, "Luckily for you, Sheikha Aisha seems to be quite a willful and headstrong young woman who'd do anything for a *friend*. Her brother agreed to give your captors an extraordinarily large sum of money."

Dhamar wasn't entirely sure if it was the pain or the knowledge that Aisha did care about him that sent a wave of giddiness through him. Who was he kidding? Of course it was the latter!

If he wasn't ready to fight for his life before, he most certainly was now. He'd never been a quitter but he had been close to giving up. Now everything shone with a sweet, promising light, a glow that was surely healing him faster than anything else possible.

"She must care about me," he said thickly. He couldn't deny it, not now she'd actually come through for him. Despite all his injuries, the revelation uplifted him and made his heart soar.

"It would appear so," the doctor said, getting rid of the needle and packing up his bag. "Without her you'd no doubt be dead. She saved your life."

"When can I see her?"

"When you're able to walk out of here. At least two or three days I'd say."

Dhamar struggled to sit. His head immediately swam, his vision blacking out around the edges before he slumped back onto the ground.

The doctor sighed heavily. "You must be really desperate to see her." He pressed a hand to Dhamar's brow. "Believe me when I say rest is your best medicine."

Dhamar shook his head. "That's where you're wrong, Doc. Aisha is my best medicine."

The effort must have been too much. Within seconds his lashes fluttered closed and darkness beckoned...along with the dreams.

His breath caught in his throat as he caught sight of Hamid's little sister. So this was Aisha, the darling of Imbranak, and the beauty everyone was talking about. He'd seen a few pictures in the papers but they didn't do justice to her true exquisiteness. She was...perfect.

That she seemed more concerned about her brother's drinking than she was about the celebration of her sixteenth birthday party was a real shame. Hamid was a grown man, he could take care of himself.

Aisha was still officially a child; she shouldn't be concerned about adult issues. But then she'd been thrust into that sphere the moment her older brother had died and then her father a handful of years later. She was probably concerned Hamid would abandon her next.

Dhamar's feet took on a mind of their own, taking him to her. She looked up and he smiled, then murmured, "Happy birthday, princess."

Her eyes widened. *"Princess?* I think you have the wrong royal."

He shook his head. "I know exactly who you are, Sheikha Aisha Al Wahed."

She blinked. "I'm not sure how you know me, but I don't believe I'd forget you if we'd met."

His blood thrummed and he smiled. "We haven't met. I'm Sheikh Dhamar Qadir of Chawait and a good friend of your family. Not that I've been around much lately."

"Too busy running your country?" she asked.

"Something like that."

"A pity the same thing couldn't be said for my brother," she said with a sniff. "Though our country somehow prospers despite his...distractions."

Dhamar lifted a brow. "Perhaps he needs a new distraction?"

She snorted as her gaze landed on yet another woman, this one from Hamid's harem if Dhamar wasn't mistaken. The woman was dressed to reveal more of her voluptuous body than cover it up, and there was an ease of familiarity as Hamid drew the woman close to him. "He has more than enough of those already."

"So it seems."

She sighed. "What about you?"

"What about me?"

"Do you have your own harem too?"

He shook his head. "No. When I find the right woman, she will be it for me."

Aisha's smile was genuine, warm. "It sounds like she will be one very lucky lady."

His chest tightened at her wistful tone. "I believe so."

An older man approached then, his gaze fixed on Aisha. "Happy birthday Sheikha Aisha," he murmured huskily. "I hope your sweet sixteenth is everything you imagined it would be and more."

He was a smooth operator, Dhamar had to give him that, but he was just as certain Aisha would see through the older man's good looks and smarmy words.

She blushed and giggled, then said, "Thank you so much. To be honest, I think my day has just got a whole lot better."

Dhamar frowned. Was she for real? The man had to be old enough to be her father. Even worse was that she'd fallen for his practiced charm.

The other man winked and said, "I'm Tabari, it's such an honor and a pleasure to meet you."

"Believe me, the pleasure is all mine." She giggled again, clearly flustered. "What is it that you do?"

"Now that is a long story."

She folded her arms and blinked prettily at him. "Well now you have me intrigued and I really want to know everything about you."

Tabari laughed, then drew her away with him through the crowd, leaving Dhamar frowning after them. He couldn't exactly kidnap her from the older man, as much as the idea had merit. She was far too young right now to do anything but watch her grow up. Then...he'd act.

In the meantime he'd grit his teeth and hope her infatuation with the older man would die a quick death.

Chapter Fifteen

Aisha paced back and forth in the grand ballroom. It was the only place she'd been able to take comfort in while she waited for Dhamar to be brought safely back home. Knowing that he'd built the ballroom because of her made her feel more...at home.

Because without Dhamar here with her the palace was empty, void of the man who made it someplace she wanted to stay. It'd already been seven days since his capture, with frantic phone calls to her brother to ensure the outrageous ransom would be paid to release him.

If Hamid had thought twice about the sum he hadn't let on. He'd paid it without question, seemingly aware how much Dhamar now meant to her. That it was also for a man he thought highly of had no doubt helped in his decision.

She exhaled softly, her heart beating unnaturally loud in her ears. It was amazing how a life and death situation put things into perspective. If she hadn't been aware of how deeply in love with Dhamar she was beforehand she knew it unquestionably now.

She wanted to marry him. She wanted to have his children. She wanted to be his everything.

Tabari had become nothing more than a faded memory. A mistake she'd almost made.

All she cared about was Dhamar and bringing him home.

Not even the enlarged photograph of him and Aisha, which he'd bought off Holly after she'd snapped them at the island restaurant, and which now hung in pride of place on the ballroom wall, appeased her. He'd paid an exorbitant amount for it, no doubt to benefit her charity. A pity it didn't also help to bring her husband back to her.

A tread sounded and she looked up to find Samaira walking through the arched doorway and onto the ballroom's tiled black and white floor. Her smile was strained, her features a little sunken. "I thought I might find you here."

Aisha ran her hands up and down her arms, though the long, dark-gray sleeves of her abaya meant her goose bumps stayed hidden. "I couldn't sleep."

"You and me both." Samaira's head was bare, her iron-gray hair still thick and lustrous under the light of the triple chandeliers. "Have you heard anything more?"

She shook her head. "Nothing." She bit her bottom lip. "Do you think he's okay?"

"I'm counting on it," Samaira admitted softly. She pressed fluttery hands to the crossover bodice of her soft pink abaya. "If something were to happen to him I just...I don't know what I'd do."

Aisha stepped toward her, folding the older woman into her arms. Samaira was surprisingly frail, but then she'd probably eaten very little this past week. Aisha clung onto the older woman as tightly as she clung onto her. "He *has* to come home," Aisha said softly.

Samaira pulled back from her with watery eyes and a little sniff, but she had no hesitation in asking, "You do really love him, don't you?"

Aisha nodded. "I do."

That it sounded like her marriage vow spoken early sent a sudden prickle of premonition through her. They *would* marry. He *would* come home! She clutched onto that hope...it was all she had.

The older woman managed a smile. "I guess you wouldn't have come up with the ransom if you didn't actually care deeply about him." She dabbed at her eyes with a tissue. "I can't thank you enough for that."

"You don't have to thank me. He would have done the same for me."

His mother laughed. "Indeed. He'd move mountains for you."

Aisha's heart lurched. "I believe you." She only wished she'd realized far earlier how deeply Dhamar cared for her and the people in his life.

Whop. Whop. Whop.

At the sound of an approaching helicopter Aisha and Samaira stared at each other for a handful of seconds. Aisha breathed, "He's here!"

Without another word they hurried out of the ballroom and down the wide corridor toward the wing of the palace where a staircase and elevator took guests to the palace roof and its helipad. Aisha took the stairs two-at-a-time while a puffed out Samaira pressed the button for the elevator.

Aisha's heart was beating out from her chest by the time she burst through the door and onto the roof. The helicopter rotors were still spinning noisily, the positional lights a blur of red, green and white.

The helicopter door was open and Manzur—the one and only man who'd been allowed to retrieve Dhamar from his captors—had already alighted. He stood bent a little beneath the rotors as he reached into the cabin to help his sheikh out.

Aisha gasped at seeing Dhamar. He refused assistance though he probably needed it. He'd always kept himself lean, corded and powerful. Now he looked...vulnerable. He'd been starved and had lost much of his muscle mass, his body battered and bruised and his nose clearly broken.

She withheld a whimper. He was lucky to be alive.

A doctor stepped forward from the shadows nearby with half-a-dozen other men who'd been waiting for his arrival. Aisha hovered back, uncertain now whether to approach with the doctor and other men surrounding him. Then Dhamar looked up. His shadowed eyes connecting with hers, he mouthed, *"Princess."*

Her legs unlocked and she stumbled toward him. He wrapped his arms around her and gazed down into her eyes, and though he was clearly weak, his words were strong when he said, "I love you."

Ding.

Samaira trotted out of the elevator, her stare widening as she took in her ravaged son. "No!" she cried out.

Dhamar put up his hand, communicating to his mother that he'd live while letting her know he needed a moment.

Aisha only distantly noticed. Her emotions were fine-tuned to the three little words that meant everything to her. That those same three words hovered on her lips but didn't get spoken had to hurt him deeply.

He didn't show it.

He studied Aisha, as though reading her emotions, his eyes flicking over her face before he caught and held her gaze. "Marry me, princess," he said hoarsely.

Aisha blinked up at him, her heart fluttering in her chest. "Yes," she said softly. As his stare moved to her lips, as though deciphering her answer over the helicopter noise, she shouted joyfully, *"Yes!"*

Chapter Sixteen

Aisha woke up with Dhamar's arms wrapped around her from behind and one of his legs thrown over hers. She smiled. He'd made it almost impossible for her to move let alone to leave him.

Not that she minded. She wanted nothing to ever separate them again.

It seemed hard to believe it'd been seven days since his return home. She lifted her left hand to admire the exquisite yellow gold engagement and wedding rings on her finger. That she was married to Dhamar now was even more surreal. But after Dhamar's surgery to fix his broken nose and fully recuperate from his infection and cracked ribs, he'd insisted they marry in a private ceremony, with only his mother, Hamid and Holly as their witnesses.

He'd promised his people there would be a month-long celebration once he'd regained full strength. The news had been enough to excite those who'd been miffed about hearing the news after the event, and placate everyone else who'd been uncertain of her as his wife.

"You're awake," Dhamar murmured throatily, one of his hands stroking her bare skin before settling over her flat stomach as though wishing for a baby would make it so.

With how often they made love she wouldn't be surprised if she *was* pregnant sooner rather than later. He might still have some muscle mass and weight to regain but it didn't stop him from pleasuring her in the bedroom. He was insatiable. He especially enjoyed it when she was on top to give his ribs a serious chance to heal.

"How did you know?"

"Other than you no longer snoring like a freight train?" At her outraged gasp he chuckled and said, "Joking, princess. I've yet to hear you snore. But even if you did I wouldn't care. I'd train myself to fall asleep like you were serenading me with a lullaby."

She snorted. "Now you're just trying to be romantic."

"Trying?"

She giggled. "Okay, okay. You *are* romantic." Her gaze slipped to the latest bouquet of flowers he'd gifted her. White lilies, baby's breath and crimson rosebuds scented the air sweetly from their vase on an occasional table.

A smile curled her lips. She loved the fact her husband had flown the bouquet in especially for her. There'd been too little time to organize flowers for their wedding so he'd promised her a new bouquet every week. She'd protested but he hadn't backed down, and she had to admit she'd been delighted when these had arrived yesterday.

She swallowed, becoming serious. "I don't even want to think about what my life would be like now without you in it."

He kissed the top of her head, and she wiggled around to face him so that they could properly kiss, while she was careful not to touch his nose. He still had a dressing on it as well as an internal splint. She'd bet he'd end up with a slightly crooked nose that would make him look even more roguishly handsome.

"You're such a good kisser," he murmured against his lips.

"I learned from the master."

He groaned. "You did." But though his erection nudged her belly, he pulled back and said, "As much as I'd love to ravish you all over again, I have someplace I need to be this morning."

"You mean other than inside me?"

His groan deepened into a growl. "I've created a monster." Giving her one last, lingering kiss, he climbed out of bed. "Meet you in an hour for breakfast?"

She rolled farther onto his side of the bed. "Can't we just cuddle instead?"

He leaned down, giving her one last peck on the lips. "Not this morning princess. I have some important business to discuss."

"Go do your sheikh stuff then." Though he grinned at her airy dismissal, there was some raw, unnamed emotion behind his stare.

Then he blinked, his honey-brown eyes looking normal once again, and she decided she'd imagined it.

He knew she knew as well as anyone that his being a sheikh and a leader was no easy matter. She'd been brought up to see how much pressure and responsibility it entailed. It had been one of the reasons Hamid had bordered on becoming an alcoholic.

She blew out a slow, long breath. "I suppose I'd better get out of bed so I can see you again shortly."

He sent her a salute, then pivoted and walked toward their walk-in closet, and for a moment she allowed herself to stare as his corded muscles rolled and flexed. He'd definitely built up some more weight since coming home, but he was still spare, his hardness even more obvious now.

He'd been through hell and he'd survived, and she couldn't be more in awe of him.

She got out of bed as soon as he stepped out of their suite of rooms. It was surreal to not only now share his bed but his life, too. It hadn't been that long ago she hadn't even seen inside his suite of rooms, now she lived in them with him.

She loved the masculine touch of his huge, dark-stained timber bed, with all the gold bedding and furnishings. Even the mosaic ceiling with its gold and blue patterned tiles brought her comfort. She didn't want to change a thing. His bedroom reminded her of Dhamar in every way.

They could live in a hut and she'd be happy. She had no doubt he'd be happy too. He'd confessed that his enforced stay with his captors had made him realize life was too short and he needed to grab what he wanted with both hands. And what he wanted, all he really wanted was her...his princess.

The feeling was mutual, despite the fact she'd yet to tell him she loved him. It was a silly superstition but she felt as though telling him what he wanted so desperately to hear would destroy their blossoming relationship...their marriage.

Taking a quick shower and getting dressed into a pale blue abaya, she braided her hair and put on her signature kohl eyeliner before she wandered back into the bedroom.

Slipping on a pair of strappy sandals, she headed out of their suite of rooms and to the intimate dining room where she and Dhamar dined most nights with his mother. This morning she and her husband would be breakfasting with her brother and his wife, Holly.

That she was thirty minutes earlier than planned didn't really occur to her until she stepped through the archway and spotted Dhamar and Hamid already seated and talking animatedly. She froze as some of their conversation filtered her way.

"You have nothing to prove. Bad enough you repaid all the ransom money I gifted you."

"It's not like I can't afford it."

"Then perhaps forget about going after those men who took you and—"

"Not an option, Hamid. When word gets out I paid the ransom, next time it might be my wife they take."

That she hadn't been imagining his hidden emotion this morning brought her no comfort. Not knowing he'd been planning something so fundamental behind her back! She forced her legs to unlock and asked in a gritty, accusing voice, "What is going on?"

Her husband and her brother looked up guiltily, before Dhamar frowned and said, "You're early."

"I am." She crossed her arms. "And I'm guessing I wasn't meant to hear this conversation?"

Hamid cleared his throat. "You must understand...everything Dhamar does he does for you."

"Does that include going to war on the men who kidnapped him?"

Hamid nodded. "It does."

Fury pulsed through her veins. "How dare you both sit here and make plans that affect me!" She stomped toward them. "We paid your ransom, Dhamar. It's over now—finished!"

His eyes glittered. "It will never be finished now, princess. It will happen again and *you* might be their next victim. And I won't see you hurt...or worse."

"Don't *princess* me! Do I have no say in this?" A tear rolled down her cheek, but it was born of fury. "Just who, exactly, is going after these people—these sadistic and dangerous criminals?" She stared at her husband. "Let me guess, *you* will be in the thick of it!"

Dhamar pushed back his chair. "What sort of a leader would I be if I sent my men into battle without me at their side?"

"A smart man!" she raged. She turned to Hamid. "Tell him not to go, Hamid! Do something!"

Hamid sighed heavily, his plaits swinging forward as he pushed a hand over his face. "It's not my decision to make."

She shook her head. "Well I didn't sign up for this!"

Dhamar's jaw tightened, giving him an even fiercer look thanks to his weight loss. "What are you saying?"

"I'm saying I don't know if I'll be here when you—*if* you—get back!"

His eyes flashed. "You know I'd scour the ends of the Earth to find you again."

Hamid stood, his expression resolute as he faced his sister. "Let's not say things we might come to regret. I know how much you adore your husband. That he's doing everything he can to make you safe shouldn't dilute your feelings toward him. It should strengthen them."

She rubbed her arms, her rage abruptly draining out of her. "I just...I nearly lost him once. I don't want to lose him again."

Dhamar stepped toward her. "Hey, I'm still here. You can talk to me."

She blinked back emotion. "Can I?" she asked, voice anguished. "Why is it I have to find out your plans by accident if we can discuss things?"

He sighed heavily. "You're right. I shouldn't hide things from you."

"But you did anyway," she said bitterly.

He clasped her shoulders. "I didn't want to worry you." His eyes darkened. "You've been through enough already."

"And yet you're ready to risk it all again."

"Yes, I am. I'm risking it all for *us*. Everything I'm doing is for us and our future."

She was vaguely aware of Holly arriving then, and of Hamid going to her and them both leaving the dining room. Giving them space. But space wasn't what she needed. Her husband was what she needed now and in her future. Her whole body quaked, the Earth shifting beneath her feet. Why couldn't he see how much she needed him?

"Hey," Dhamar said quietly. "I know you suffer from fear of abandonment, but I'm not going to leave you, okay?"

"How do you know that?" she whispered brokenly. "How do I know you'll come back home to me?"

"All I ask is that you trust me, okay? I've put measures in place and thought out every strategy and outcome possible. In three more days this will be all behind us and we'll be living our own happily ever after." He lifted his hands from her shoulders to cup her face. "I love you, princess. I won't betray your trust. I just want us to have a future together. A *safe* future."

She closed her eyes, swaying toward him but still unable to say the three words back to him. Especially not now he was putting himself at risk and testing his luck. "I want that too," she admitted softly.

He exhaled with a long suffering sigh, clearly unsettled by her reluctance to love him openly and without reservation. But then he enclosed her in his arms and she was lost to him.

Lost to whatever fate decided.

Chapter Seventeen

Three days later, Aisha was ready to tear her hair out, or scream, preferably both. She'd been walking non-stop through the palace and was all but lost in the wing she assumed was meant for the servants or guests. She couldn't handle the waiting game any longer. Dhamar and his men had left in the early hours of the morning long before sunrise. They'd been gone—what?—ten hours, twelve?

She unconsciously twisted the bridal set on her finger. She should have had word by now!

She was only glad her brother was no longer involved. He and Holly had flown back to Imbranak yesterday, making them one less thing for Aisha to worry about. Not that it stopped the fear from careening through her chest. Dhamar wasn't yet fully recovered. It'd be so easy for him to slip up and make a mistake.

She pivoted, then covered her face in her hands. She had to get out of here! She had to do something...*anything* or she'd go crazy imagining the worst!

She dropped her hands and blinked up into the huge dome skylight, where leaded glass refracted the late afternoon sun and bounced off the spines of hundreds of books in their shelves. The natural light was perfect for reading. But though she would have loved discovering this library by accident at any other given moment, no book was going to distract her now.

She needed to saddle up Black Zippy and go for a ride. She needed to lose herself in a gallop, with the wind in her hair and adrenaline pumping through her blood.

Her mind made up, she left the library at a run, speeding through the corridors then until she finally found a way outside through a back entrance of the palace. It was easy enough from there to find the big rectangular block of stables.

Arabian horses hung their heads out of their stalls at hearing her approach, but all she cared about was finding her black filly. Until Smoke whickered greeting and she paused for just a moment to stroke his broad head. "It's good to see you're recovered and doing so well. Maybe you can come with me and Black Zippy on our next ride."

She wouldn't—couldn't—think about Dhamar not coming back and taking Smoke for that ride. It was unthinkable.

A stablehand appeared and quickly saddled up Black Zippy before leading her out. The young man seemed too awed to question that she was riding alone. He probably imagined as a sheikha she made her own rules.

She resisted laughing. If only he knew! In some ways she was more repressed than the lowliest of women.

Thankful she'd worn leggings under her abaya, she swung up onto the filly then walked her along the front of the stalls toward the decorative wall where a small gate allowed Dhamar and his guests to come and go from the stables on their chosen mounts.

She lifted her chin. As Dhamar's wife the guards would surely allow her to pass?

A guard stepped forward, his stare flinty and suspicious. "I'm sorry, I can't allow you to ride out of here unescorted."

Her shoulders tensed, and the filly immediately tossed her head, sensing her sudden anxiety. "Do you know who I am?" she asked imperiously. "My brother is Sheikh of Imbranak. My husband is Sheikh of Chawait—*your* sheikh."

The man's face paled, while a second guard poked his head out of the door of the hut where they were stationed, then as quickly withdrew. The guard in front of her cleared his throat. "My apologies Sheikha Aisha. I didn't recognize you."

"Then let's hope you recognize me next time." She held his stare. "Now let me past."

"Of course." He quickly dropped his gaze and unlatched the gate. It swung open and he stepped aside and said, "Enjoy your ride."

She nodded, adjusting her hijab. "Thank you, I will." She glanced up at the clear sky, the sun already descending toward the mountainous far horizon. She'd have three or four hours at best before sundown. "I'll be back before dark."

"I'll wait here until you return."

She guided Black Zippy through the gap, then gave her a looser rein. The filly moved into a long-legged trot that quickly put distance between them and the palace with its decorative white walls. A canter put even more distance between them, until the huge palace was nothing more than a speck behind them.

A grin breaking out on Aisha's face, she leaned forward and gave Black Zippy her head. The filly didn't disappoint, surging into a gallop that caused the wind to whistle past Aisha's face and the sand beneath to blur beneath the filly's hooves.

Aisha closed her eyes and let out an exhilarated *yip*. This was just what she needed! Nothing, except sex with her husband, beat this unrestricted freedom and joy.

Dhamar had put himself in very real danger by going after the men who'd kidnapped him. Those same men wouldn't surrender. She had no doubt they'd fight to the death rather than go to jail or be sentenced to death. It meant they had nothing to lose. If they were going down, they'd bring Dhamar down with them.

Her joy dissipating fast, she opened her eyes simultaneously to a serpent just ahead in the sand uncoiling and raising its hooded head in a warning to strike. Black Zippy snorted and jumped clear of the snake.

Aisha wasn't prepared for the sudden change of pace and direction. She slid forward and then to the side, losing her seat completely. A sharp crack sounded and her head went numb, before everything went dark.

Chapter Eighteen

Dhamar sank into the back seat of the helicopter with a weary, but satisfied smile. Fatigue might be threatening to drag him under but he wouldn't allow that just yet. Not until he was reunited with his wife and he'd kissed her soft lips, then reassured her that nothing would separate them ever again.

Not if he could help it. Lord only knew he'd done everything in his power now to make them safe.

The fight on the mountain between his once-captors and he and his men had been brutal, but in the end good had prevailed. Dhamar had counted on Issam's refusal to surrender. Dhamar had also made sure he'd been the one to push a blade through the other man's black heart.

Dhamar wasn't a vindictive man, but he did whatever needed to be done for his people and his country. He did a whole lot more for the people he was close to...the people he loved. If that meant getting his hands dirty to protect his wife then so be it. He still had a clean conscience, and that meant everything in the bigger scheme of things.

He just wished all of his men had survived the carnage. Two had passed away from their wounds before their enemy had surrendered after many more of them had died.

Dhamar sighed heavily. Though he was triumphant, it was never easy losing someone. In the end there was little more he could do for the two men's families other than to adequately compensate them and pay them his respects.

The helicopter began its descent and he peered out the window to the lit-up palace below. A surge of adrenaline pushed him wide awake, accelerating his heartbeat. Aisha would be worried sick.

The landing light illuminated the helipad beneath, and a pang of disappointment hit hard at not seeing his wife waiting on the roof for him. Was she still mad at him? His breath caught in his throat. Had she actually left him like she'd threatened she would?

No. She'd come to accept his reasoning, had known it was the best thing long term. He got things done, he always had. It was a trait even she had to acknowledge was a good thing.

He was smiling when the pilot set the helicopter down smoothly. The next thing on Dhamar's "to do" list was to pleasure his wife and hear her gasps and moans as she came undone. He was never too weary for that particular scenario.

It wasn't until he climbed out and a guard approached to inform him of the latest news, that Dhamar's smile died a quick death. "What do you mean she's not here?"

The guard's face paled and Dhamar dragged the man with him as he stalked away from the noisy helicopter rotors and into the stairwell where he could hear more clearly.

The guard managed to hold Dhamar's stare. "She rode her horse outside the palace grounds and didn't return."

"She went out alone?" Dhamar gritted out.

The guard swallowed heavily, the dull lights that illuminated the stairs also highlighting his fear. "That's what I was told." He cleared his throat. "But there is a search party looking for her as we speak."

Fury burned through Dhamar. Heads would roll for this! But first he had to find his wife. "What of her horse?"

"It didn't return either."

So she was either still out riding and was likely lost, or she'd had an accident and possibly been unseated. Even the most skilled rider could take a fall. Black Zippy had been trained not to gallop home if her rider had a fall.

What if she's been the one kidnapped this time? What if her captors don't want a ransom and instead want to send a message?

Fear careened through him, and he crossed his arms to still the shakiness in his limbs. Tiredness was a distant memory now. "Send out a bigger search party, with as many men that can be spared as possible," he commanded. "I'll have my pilot take me up in the air and search from up high."

He didn't wait around to watch the guard hurry off to do his bidding. Dhamar was already stalking back toward the helicopter to bark out instructions to the pilot. As the helicopter lifted back into the air again, Dhamar's whole body was coiled tight.

If he didn't find his wife, he'd never forgive himself.

Chapter Nineteen

Aisha was dreaming, she was certain of it. Her father had died years ago, no doubt from the devastating loss of his eldest son, and yet here he was looking down at her with his face filled with concern. She frowned as he smiled reassurance. He'd only ever loved Ardon. He'd certainly never shown her or Hamid any love or affection.

Whop. Whop. Whop.

Aisha blinked into the sudden wash of light even as her father disappeared, as though his every molecule dissolved the closer and brighter the light shone.

"Dad, don't go," she croaked. She might never have felt loved by him, yet his one vestige of concern had filled her heart to bursting.

A shame it was too little, too late.

A helicopter with its spotlight made everything around her as bright as sunlight, the glare making her flinch and close her eyes, while the dull ache at her brow thumped harder than ever.

A horse snorted and she shielded her eyes to see Black Zippy standing a few yards away. The filly's eyes were wild and she was trembling and clearly terrified, but she didn't gallop away.

Her trainer had done an exemplary job with her.

Wait. What *was* Black Zippy doing there?

What am I doing here?

She gasped as everything abruptly flooded back. Her husband was in real danger and she'd undoubtedly put herself in danger too. She tried to sit but everything swirled around her, all illumination dimming to black.

The next time she woke it was to Dhamar shouting her name before he crouched beside her, his gaze trawling over her. "You're hurt." His ragged voice betrayed his emotions.

She resisted touching her throbbing head. She'd fallen off her horse. She must have hit her head on a rock. It'd still been daylight then, which meant she'd likely been out to it for hours. "I shouldn't have gone off on my own."

"No, you shouldn't," he agreed heavily. Ripping off the hem of his thobe, he wrapped it gently around her head. "I'm going to carry you to the helicopter now and get my doctor to check you over. Do you think you'll be okay?"

She nodded, then winced. It was as if her brain was moving at a different speed to her skull. "What about Black Zippy?"

"My men on the ground are on their way even as we speak. They'll bring her home."

She blinked again. It hurt so much just to keep her eyes open. But it was suddenly imperative that she tell him her feelings. "Dhamar, I—"

"Just relax, princess." He picked her up carefully and held her against his chest, the spotlight and the still-spinning helicopter blades making her brain hurt. "You need to get fully checked over."

Her chest expanded with anxiety. Like if she didn't tell him the truth right here and now she'd lose him...for good this time. "Dhamar. I love you."

He froze, his expression unreadable.

Disappointment bit deep. Had he changed his mind about her? Did he regret bringing her with him now? Was she too much trouble? Her throat felt too thick suddenly, all her insecurities and past abandonment issues coming to the fore. She'd never be his perfect princess. She was too unconventional, too outspoken and stubborn.

Then his breath whooshed out and his eyes burned. He bent his head, his voice cracking with emotion into her ear. "That means everything to me, princess."

All her fears faded, her chest aching and her eyes watering. "*You* mean everything to me."

His grip tightened fractionally, then he was striding toward the helicopter and boarding it with her still in his arms. He didn't let her go once he took his seat. Either he knew she couldn't stay upright, or he simply didn't want to part from her again. That she believed it was the latter sent her heart soaring.

The helicopter roared as it lifted, then she closed her eyes with a wide smile and gave into the need to simply lose all awareness.

She next woke as her husband lowered her gently onto their bed. He smiled down at her, tenderness making his eyes soft. "The doctor is waiting to see you."

Of course, Dhamar would have ensured nothing less. "Okay," she said hoarsely.

A young, bearded man in a white coat with a stethoscope hanging from his neck stepped forward. It all seemed so cliché she couldn't help but giggle, then winced at the tight feeling of her brain against her skull.

The doctor took in her reaction and he quickly took charge, wrapping the cuff of a blood pressure machine around her arm and checking the numbers before he took off his stethoscope and listened to her heart. "Blood pressure is a little high, but that is to be expected." He unwrapped the makeshift bandage from her head and carefully cleaned the cut on the back of her head. "I'll need to take some x-rays and stitch you up."

She nodded as he wheeled a portable x-ray machine to her bedside and proceeded with the required images. Twenty minutes later he'd finished stitching up her head wound and seemed satisfied with her general health.

He turned to Dhamar. "I'll come back tomorrow morning to monitor her again. But with the possibility of concussion, I'd suggest a couple of days bedrest."

"Can I at least take a shower?" she asked. Sand was stuck in her hair and her clothes, along with blood from her head wound.

"Of course. Just keep your stitches dry and clean," the doctor advised.

It wasn't until he'd grabbed his bag and the blood pressure machine, and an assistant wheeled out the portable x-ray machine, that her husband lifted her off the bed and said, "Let's take that shower."

She didn't complain when he carried her into the adjoining bathroom, then set her onto her feet and gently undressed her. She didn't even complain when he retrieved a shower cap from the bathroom cabinet drawer and covered her head wound.

She glanced into the mirror. She looked ridiculous, yet he gazed at her like she was the most beautiful woman on the planet.

He pushed a hand over his face. "I thought I might have lost you today. I was scared stiff you were taken or killed to avenge all those men who kept me captive and who I had killed or imprisoned."

"Then you understand now how worried I was about you and what you did to keep us safe."

He nodded. "Yes. And I never want to go through that again."

"Neither do I," she admitted in a small voice.

He cupped her face and reverently kissed her. "I love you."

"I love you, too."

His breath hissed. "I thought it might have been concussion earlier when you spoke those same words."

"It wasn't. I've known for a while, I was just too scared to admit my feelings. I thought telling you the truth might ruin everything." She bit her bottom lip. "I'm not superstitious, but I was so scared our marriage would fail if I became too confident, too optimistic."

His eyes darkening, he stepped into the shower and turned on the water. Adjusting the temperature before he undressed, he then drew her into the stall with him. The water crashed against her shower cap, but as he soaped up her body with gentle hands, she could hear his murmured reassurances.

"I won't ever abandon you or do you wrong. Trust that I'll never let you down."

Her whole body trembled with need by the time he'd finished soaping up every inch of her while erasing her fears. He rinsed off the soap then washed himself quickly before turning off the spray. Despite his arousal, he didn't make a move, instead he took off her shower cap and used a facecloth to gently wipe away any dried blood on her scalp, then he drew her out onto the fluffy mat where he proceeded to dry her.

She giggled a little when he kissed the tip of her nose, then carried her back into the bedroom and laid her on the bed. Climbing in beside her, he drew her close and said, "Banish your fears, princess. You are my one and only."

She shivered a little at his words, then admitted, "And you are my everything."

His breath shuddered out. "I love you, princess. Now and forever."

As he drew her back to his front so that they fitted perfectly together, she realized she'd never been happier. She trusted him as much as she loved him. And she'd do everything possible to enjoy each day they were given together.

Epilogue

Six weeks later...

Aisha leaned forward on Black Zippy as they followed the zigzag trail up the mountain. Dhamar rode his stallion, Smoke, just in front of them, his stallion's white tail swishing and hooves clattering as they forged ahead.

Shade dappled the path, the trills of bird song and the buzzing of red dwarf bees filling the air. She guessed there must be a hive nearby as the scent of honey was almost cloying, making her nose twitch.

They were getting close to the top of the mountain when Smoke broke into a powerful, long-legged trot. Aisha grinned as she gave Black Zippy a loose rein, allowing her to follow pace. Then the incline suddenly leveled out, the trees thinning to reveal a drop off in front, which showcased the desert vista spread out before them.

Her breath caught as she reined Black Zippy to a stop beside Smoke. "Oh, wow. That is spectacular."

Dhamar smiled proudly, pointing to where the palace gleamed under the blazing sun in the distance. "And there's our home."

Even from afar the size of the palace blew her mind. She'd yet to explore it fully. But from up here, with the desert sands glaring an off-white color and the palace glowing bright white, she, too, was proud of this desolate piece of paradise.

An eagle soared up high, as weightless as air, its outspread wings giving it a freedom she could only dream of. Not that she'd change a thing. Being with Dhamar, being married to him, she'd never been happier or more content. Love was all that mattered. Love was everything.

Smoke sidled a little closer to Black Zippy and Dhamar grinned and said, "It's quite the view, isn't it."

"It sure is." Her grin matched his when he reached for her hand and held it.

"No regrets?" he asked gently.

She squeezed his hand. "You need to ask?"

"Remember I've had four years of watching you yearn for another man."

"And at least a few days of me hating you for taking away my dream man," she added with an arched brow.

He grimaced. "Yes, that too."

It was kind of reassuring to know she hadn't been alone in her insecurities, and that even her great sheikh husband wasn't infallible with his emotions. "I wouldn't change what you and I have now for the world." A surge of emotion swept through her. "What your mother said to me is true. You really would move mountains for me."

"I would," he said. "And climb them all with you too."

The eagle cried out then, an echo that might have been agreement.

"I know that now," she said softly. "You won't abandon me. You'll do whatever you have to in order to keep me safe and happy." She pressed his hand to her heart, and then farther down against her stomach. "To keep your family safe."

When his honey-gold eyes widened, then darkened with emotion, she knew she couldn't have surprised him more if she tried. Her doctor had only just confirmed the news to her last night and had advised her that horse-riding and most other activities were fine at this early stage.

She'd hugged the news to herself while waiting for Dhamar to return from a meeting with some of their country's dignitaries. She'd fallen asleep before he'd returned, and had decided this morning she'd give him the news someplace special and in complete privacy. There was nowhere more private or special than up here on the mountain with glorious views of his palace and its surrounds.

Drawing in a shuddery breath, he asked, "We're having a baby?"

She nodded, her voice shaky with emotion. "Yes."

His gleeful shout echoed around them, louder than any eagle's. He leaned closer to her, his mouth closing over hers in a kiss that was surprisingly intimate considering they were on horseback. When he finally pulled away, the horses standing obediently still, he whispered, "I'm going to be a father."

She nodded, her eyes filling with happy tears. "You're going to be the best dad in the world."

"And you'll be the best mom in the world," he said reverently. Tightening his hold on her hand, he said, "Let's go home, princess."

Want more Desert King's Alliance stories by Mel Teshco...
The Sheikh's Fake Fiancée

She's an outcast. He's a newly appointed sheikh. It can't possibly work—can it?

Zania Akhtar has only one regret in life: falling for the smooth lies and seduction of an older man, the same man her once best friend and Sheikha of Imbranak imagined herself in love with. Now Zania is scorned by her friends and strangers alike, and with no money and apparently even less values, she has no one to turn to—until Sheikh Kain Al Hadi of Dumak, proposes an idea to her.

Sheikh Kain Al Hadi is in a dilemma. Not only is his beloved widowed mother desperate for him to marry and create heirs to the throne, he can't keep his eyes off a young and beautiful commoner whose reputation is in absolute tatters. There is only one thing for it—a fake engagement. It will restore Zania's reputation while getting his mother off his back about marriage and babies. Then once the dust settles, his libido is quenched and her mother realizes her mistake, he and Zania can go their separate ways.

But things don't always go according to plan.

Chapter One of the Sheikh's Fake Fiancée

Zania Akhtar stared unseeingly at the ocean's beautiful blue vista spread out below her while tears streamed down her face. Thankfully, no one was here to see her cry and no one would care even if they were here.

She was an outcast, a pariah to her closest friends after she'd fallen for the smooth lies of a man she'd truly believed had loved her. And now here she was on the beautiful Holly Island, abandoned and rejected...and never more alone.

Despite the midday heat, she shivered. She'd been holding it together pretty well until just now. She'd been hiding out here on the resort, taking advantage of Sheikh Hamid's hospitality in letting her stay longer while she kept the media at bay and Sheikh Kain Al Hadi at arm's length.

Kain.

She didn't quite believe his interest in her, particularly now her character was in such disrepute. But then she no longer believed in anything or anyone...not anymore. She no longer even trusted in herself let alone another man.

The newspaper article she'd read just minutes ago in her room only confirmed it. She was to blame for Sheikha Aisha's sudden getaway to another country, just as she was to blame for Tabari's exile from Holly Island.

Not only had she lost her best friend, she'd lost the one man she'd considered herself in love with.

She'd never trust anyone again.

"There you are."

She swung around with a sharp gasp, facing the one man she'd been trying to avoid. At seeing her tears his gaze narrowed, his shoulders stiffening. *Shit.* The last thing she wanted or needed was his sympathy.

"Kain." She sniffed, her chin lifting. "I should have known you'd find me."

"Oh, I knew you were here," he said quietly. "I was just giving you some space."

Her shoulders tensed, her eyes burning harder still. Had he been watching her all this time? "Well you can go now." There was never going to be enough space between her and every other man on the planet. "I want to be alone."

"Not happening, shortcake."

How did his refusal raise such simultaneous sweet relief and bitter revolt? She glowered. Either way, she might be small but she was no longer a pushover. She'd learned from that mistake. "What do you want from me?"

"We've discussed that already, remember?" He stepped closer and she resisted taking a step back, though the thought of tumbling off the cliff edge and into the churning waves of the abyss below held sudden appeal. As though he'd read her mind, his eyes darkened, caution edging them. "Pretend to be my fiancée and solve both our problems."

She dragged the back of her hand across her face, swiping dry her tears. "I'm sure any number of women would love to play the role of your fiancée. You hardly need me for that."

"See that's where you're wrong. I don't care about any other number of women, but I do care about you. The way I see it, you have nothing more to lose and everything to gain. And being that I'm obviously attracted to you I won't need to pretend to want you."

That he admitted being attracted to her did something to her insides and somehow dulled the sharp agony of Tabari's betrayal.

"I-I'm no actress," she admitted.

"And yet you put on a brave face the entire time your name was being dragged through the mud."

She trembled. He was right. She'd kept her head high and her eyes dry while everyone had gossiped and talked cruelly about her. Even her best friend, Sheikha Aisha, the one and same woman she'd respected and loved above all others, had turned her back on her. And who could blame her? For the first time in Zania's life she'd thought of herself first and her best friend second.

That the man Zania and Aisha had trusted implicitly had turned out to be a selfish, unworthy rat was too little too late. Zania had given Tabari her heart along with her body and now she was the one who paid the ultimate price.

But though her virginity might have been taken along with her dignity and self-respect, she refused to give up her pride. She'd walk over hot coals with her chin held high if that was what it took. No one needed to know she was hurting inside and quaking with anxiety.

"It's hot out here," Kain added softly. "Why don't you get out of the sun and join me for lunch? I've ordered room service with enough food for two."

Her stomach growled fitfully even as she lied and said, "I'm not really hungry."

"You need to eat, shortcake. You'll fade away if you're not careful."

She sighed heavily. He was right. At five foot two and already on the slender side she couldn't afford to starve herself. "Just a quick bite."

She clapped a hand to her mouth when she walked into his suite of rooms a few minutes later and saw the hamburgers sitting on plates, a bowl of hot fries to share on the side. There were even two different milkshakes, one a frothy caramel the other a strawberry flavor. "How did you know?" she breathed.

He winked. "That hamburgers were your favorite meal ever?" When she nodded, he explained, "I heard you went overseas to Australia as a teenager and adored the food over there, most especially the hamburgers. I thought you might appreciate them here too."

Why did his finding out that about her and acting on it make her feel so much better? She hurried over to the table and took the top off one of the burgers. "No way! They even have beetroot and pineapple on them."

He grinned, his eyes sparkling. "They do."

She put the top back on then sat and picked up the burger, leaning over the plate while she took a big bite of the meat patty with sauce and salad. "Oh!" she closed her eyes. "Delicious!"

He joined her at the table with a low chuckle. "I was going to be a gentleman and pull out a chair for you, but watching you eat is even more satisfying."

She smiled. Impossible as it seemed, sitting with him in his suite of rooms while eating delicious hamburgers really was lifting her spirits. He might be a sheikh but he was incredibly easy to talk to. Perhaps because she'd been brought up around sheikhs and sheikhas all her life and saw them as everyday people.

Just don't do anything to wrong them or shame and humiliate them in any way and you'll be okay.

A pity it was too late to take back what she'd done to Sheikha Aisha. Zania just hoped her best friend would eventually forgive her and realize not only did it take two to tango, but that Zania had been stupidly susceptible and blinded by Tabari's flattery and persuasive charm.

She placed her half-eaten hamburger back onto the plate. "That was delicious. Thank you."

Kain picked up the bowl of fries and proffered them to her. "I hope you've saved room for a few of these."

She selected two and ate them delicately. Despite loving fries with her burgers, after eating very little these last few days it was an effort to eat more than a few mouthfuls of anything.

It wasn't until Kain had finished his burger and he'd wiped his mouth and hands on a napkin that he leaned back and said, "I'm glad we finally caught up."

She took a sip of the caramel shake, her lashes fluttering at the rich, creamy taste. "Oh?"

He picked up the strawberry shake with a grin, then sucked some down through a straw. "I wanted you to know I'm leaving Holly Island tomorrow."

The milk suddenly soured in her stomach and she pressed a hand there and asked weakly, "You are?"

He nodded. "I've been fobbing off some important matters for long enough already."

"Then of course you must go."

How odd was it that she'd wanted so desperately to be left alone, yet the moment Kain said he was leaving her whole body shut down in denial.

He leaned forward, his big hand moving to rest on her thigh. She shivered in awareness. The thin fabric of her pink abaya was no match for the powerful magnetism he exuded. He was nothing short of a big cat stalking its prey. She swallowed hard. If he was a tiger in the jungle then Tabari had been a crying kitten dumped in an alley.

"You should come with me," he murmured huskily. "I don't want you here alone."

She bit her bottom lip. "I honestly don't know what I should do anymore."

"What have you got to lose? Accept my offer." He leaned closer, his other hand reaching out to cup her jaw and keep her gaze locked onto his. "Do you even have a home to return to?"

She stared. *Holy shit.* She hadn't really thought about that. Had Aisha kicked her out of the palace? She had nowhere else to go, no one else to turn to. Even her mother, who'd been one of Aisha's many nannies when she'd been a child, was now in an aged care facility and barely knew her own name anymore.

She closed her eyes. At least her mother wouldn't learn about the shameful behavior of her daughter.

His hand tightened its grip and her eyes flicked open to find his intent, brilliant dark stare on hers. "All I ask is that you act the part of being my fiancée and pretend you're totally in love with me."

She tried not to breathe in his smoky cypress and amber scent, but she adored men's fragrances and his was clearly unique and no doubt hideously expensive. Her nostrils flared as she secretly indulged her craving. That his request could be fulfilled by any other number of beautiful women didn't seem to matter to him. He wanted her to act the role and no one else would do.

She cleared her throat, her whole body tingling at his touch, his scent. "H-how long will I need to keep up the charade?"

"One month. By that time your name will be exonerated and my mother should realize having a daughter-in-law and grandbabies is no longer her greatest wish after all. Then you and I can go our separate ways and no one will be any the wiser." He dropped his hand. "You will, of course, be adequately compensated for your trouble and your time."

Zania blew out a slow, considered breath. If she really did no longer have a home then any money would be a blessing. And it wasn't as if she had to kiss a toad. Kain was a little too easy on the eyes. That being with him might salvage her reputation helped make up her mind.

"What do you say?" he prompted huskily.

She blinked at him. Then swallowing back any doubts, she answered, "I say—yes."

If you'd like to know when my next book is available, as well as other pre-orders, cover reveals and other news, sign up for my newsletter: https://madmimi.com/signups/121695/join

Check out my website – http://www.melteshco.com/

You can also friend me on Facebook at https://www.facebook.com/mel.teshco

Or my author Facebook page at https://www.facebook.com/MelTeshcoAuthor

Contact me: melteshco@yahoo.com.au

If you enjoy my books I'd be delighted if you would consider leaving a review. This will help other readers find my books ☺

About the Author

I'm an award winning author who loves to write scorching hot contemporary and science fiction romance—stories I love to read. I love working from home, where my office window looks out over our 'block' of fourteen acres with gorgeous mountain views. After enjoying a stint as a foster carer for cats, I now have seven felines to entertain me, along with two dogs and two horses. But only when I'm not distracted by my three gorgeous daughters, one of whom—a teenager *shriek*—is still living at home. As for my husband...he's still waiting for retirement.

Want more Mel Teshco books?

Contemporary

Desert Kings Alliance

The Sheikh's Runaway Bride (book 1)

The Sheikh's Captive Lover (book 2)

The Sheikh's Forbidden Wife (book 3)

The Sheikh's Secret Mistress (book 4)

The Sheikh's Defiant Princess (book 5)

The Sheikh's Fake Fiancée (book 6)

The Sheikh's Royal Widow (book 7)

The Sheikh's Temporary Girlfriend (book 8)

Desert Kings Alliance Box Set (Volumes 1-4)

Desert Kings Alliance Box Set (Volumes 5-8)

Gangsters at War

Wedlocked (book 1)

Avenged (book 2)

Enforced (book 3)

Contracted (book4)

more coming soon...

Bachelor Brothers of Sydney

Highest Bid (book 1)

Bought at Auction (book 2)

Winning Offer (book 3)

The VIP Desire Agency

Lady in Red (book 1)

High Class (book 2)

Exclusive (book 3)

Liberated (book 4)

Uninhibited (book 5)

The VIP Desire Agency Boxed Set (all 5 books in the series)

Box sets with authors Christina Phillips & Cathleen Ross

Sheikhs & Billionaires

Taken by the Sheikh

Taken by the Billionaire

Taken by the Desert Sheikh

Resisting the Firefighter

Standalone longer length titles: (50k-100k)

As I Am

Standalone novellas and short stories: (15k-40K)

Stripped

Clarissa

Camilla

Selena's Bodyguard (also part of the Christmas Assortment Box)

Anthologies

Down and Dusty: The Complete Collection

The Christmas Assortment Box

Science Fiction

The Virgin Hunt Games

The Virgin Hunt Games volume 1

The Virgin Hunt Games volume 2

The Virgin Hunt Games volume 3

The Virgin Hunt Games volume 4

The Virgin Hunt Games volume 5

The Virgin Hunt Games volume 6

Alien Fugitives

Nero (book 1)

Jasper (book 2)

Sienna (book 3)

Damaris (book 4)

Dragons of Riddich

Kadin (prequel - book 1)

Asher (book 2)

Baron (book 3)

Dahlia (book 4)

Wyatt (book 5)
Valor (book 6)
The Queen (book 7)
Alien Hunger
Galactic Burn (book 1)
Galactic Inferno (book 2)
Galactic Flame (book 3)
Coming soon
Galactic Blaze (book 4)
Nightmix
Lusting the Enemy (book 1)
Abducting the Princess (book 2)
Seducing the Huntress (book 3)
Winged & Dangerous
Stone Cold Lover (book 1)
Ice Cold Lover (book 2)
Red Hot Lover (book 3)
Winged & Dangerous Box Set (all 3 books in the series)
Dirty Sexy Space continuity with Denise Rossetti:
Yours to Uncover (book 1)
Mine to Serve (book 6)
Ours to Share (book 8)
Awakenings series with Kylie Sheaffe
No Ordinary Gift (book 1)
Believe (book 2)
Homecoming (book 3)
Standalone longer length titles: (50k-100k)
Dimensional
Mutant Unveiled
Shadow Hunter
Existence
Standalone novellas and short stories: (15k-40K)

Identity Shift
Moon Thrall
Blood Chance
Carnal Moon